FILTHY LU

Beryl Bainbridge was born in the 1930s in Liverpool and spent her early working years there as a juvenile character actress in repertory. She started writing seriously when she left the theatre behind to have her first baby.

She has written many highly-praised novels, including *The Dressmaker*, which was runner-up for the Booker Prize, and *The Bottle Factory Outing*, also a Booker Prize runner-up and winner of the *Guardian* fiction prize. *Injury Time* won the Whitbread Award in 1977. She also writes for television. *English Journey* was a BBC television series.

Beryl Bainbridge now lives in Camden Town, London, in a house full of Victorian bric-a-brac and old photographs, which she collects.

also by Beryl Bainbridge

Harriet Said
The Dressmaker
The Bottle Factory Outing
Sweet William
A Quiet Life
Injury Time
Young Adolf
Another Part of the Wood
Winter Garden
A Weekend with Claude
English Journey *(travel)*
Watson's Apology
Mum and Mr Armitage

FILTHY LUCRE

or
The Tragedy of Ernest Ledwhistle and
Richard Soleway

a story by
Beryl Bainbridge
written June to August 1946

Flamingo
Published by Fontana Paperbacks

First published in Great Britain
by Gerald Duckworth & Co. Ltd 1986

This Flamingo edition
first published by Fontana Paperbacks
8 Grafton Street, London W1X 3LA, 1988

Flamingo is an imprint
of Fontana Paperbacks, part of
the Collins Publishing Group

Made and printed in Great Britain
by William Collins Sons & Co. Ltd, Glasgow

the Family

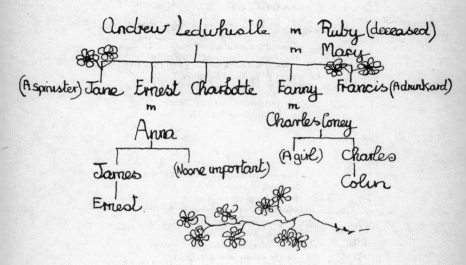

Andrew Ledwhistle m Ruby (deceased)

m Mary

(A spinster) Jane Ernest Charlotte Fanny Francis (A drunkard)

Ernest m Anna

James (No one important)

Ernest

Fanny m Charles Coney

(A girl) Charles

Colin

The Firm

Richard Andromikey   partnered   Francis Ledwhistle

Peter   "   Andrew

Martin (alias   Ernest
Richard Soloway)

Dedication

To the author of Dismal
England, who gave me a
chance to clothe my bitter
feelings against the unjust
London of the 1800's in a
story

I hope this book will useful be
And when you read it remember
me.
B. Bainbridge. August 18th. 1946.

Preface

My father and mother bickered a lot, which is why, there being no such thing as television to distract one, or any other room in which to escape from the raised voices, my mother encouraged my natural inclination to scribble in notebooks.

I had begun to write stories when I was eight years old – about an old sea-dog called Cherry Blossom Bill who kept his rum supply in his wooden leg. This was not unusual; most of my school-friends kept diaries, wrote poems or composed little playlets, though these had mainly to do with fairies living inside marigolds. Writing was more beneficial an occupation to us than attending a psychiatric clinic, should such a place have existed, and helped to get rid of anxieties nurtured by the particularly restricted sort of upbringing common to lower-class girls in wartime England. It says a lot for my mother that she was always more than ready to clear the table so that I could get down to my next chapter. If I worked for more than two hours she would say, 'Run out into the garden, pet. All authors must play.'

I had begun a novel when I was ten, but circumstances had forced me to destroy it before it was completed. I had bought a book on Livingstone's travels in Africa, a volume as big as a family bible, its pages tipped with gold leaf. I wrote my epic on pieces of exercise paper and glued them with flour-and-water paste to the existing pages. Apart from the sacrilege of defacing such a beautiful book, this attempt at secrecy was useless. In no time at all the flour swelled and the book refused to close. I was alarmed that my mother would find it and read the contents – it was an in-depth account of what I thought of her life with my father – and I didn't want to hurt her. I coated the book with dripping, put it in the bin on the path at the side of the house and set light to it. The back door caught fire.

For three years I contented myself with writing short stories to do with a lonely boy who roamed the seashore talking to seagulls. I repeated sentences in the manner of D.H. Lawrence and grew lyrical about the dark blood of the senses. Then I saw *The Thief of Bagdad* at the local picture house and launched into more exotic, carpet-flying tales.

It seemed to me, even then, that a short story was a waste of a good idea, and so I began *Filthy Lucre*. It owes a lot, undeniably, to Dickens and to Robert Louis Stevenson, two authors I was reading at the time. The character of the legless Robert Straffordson is obviously one up on Long John Silver.

I was dissatisfied with the result, mainly because it wasn't 'real life' and I had invented the characters and the plot. I don't think I have ever invented anything since. Reading it now I am of the opinion that writing is very like music, in the sense that if you hear a song often enough it becomes impossible not to go on humming the same tune. I also feel that I must have had a macabre sense of humour, because the best bits – personally speaking – have to do with either death or murder. I don't remember reading anything about the Chinese Opium War, although my father was always raving about the Yellow Peril, and I can't think where I got such a puritanical view of drinking. My poor father and mother hardly touched a drop except for a port-and-lemon at Christmas.

The spelling has been corrected – I can't spell even now – but the commas and all that are as in the original. The drawings were too frail to reproduce and are up-to-date copies of those done at the time. For the rest, it is interesting to note that in the past the influence of the written word was every bit as pervasive as the television images of the present.

B.B.

Chapter 1

A small coal fire burnt in the wide horse-and-cart grate. It was a murky evening in 1851. The old man bent over his books. His head, lit by three candles, was a grizzled white. His coat was black and dusty, his neckcloth an uninspired blue. Now and then his lips would move frettishly and he would pull his beard worriedly. Once he sighed. Then he looked round the little office at the high stool, the bundles of envelopes, the red-backed books on the shelf high above the picture of the founder of the firm of Andromikey & Ledwhistle. His eyes wandered lovingly over the brass coal-scuttle that shone like a buttercup, the threadbare carpet, the nail on the door on which his top hat rested, the files on the junior clerk's desk, the quill pens in the ginger jar. He sighed again and resumed his work. The clock on the church in Pentworth Street struck the hour.

'Ten,' he muttered. 'Ten.' He straightened, swept a bundle of papers into his pocket, blew the candles out and reached for his hat. 'I should have brought me overcoat,' he mumbled. 'Serve me right if it don't.'

The door shut and he walked slowly down the stairs. He opened the big door and went out into the street and beckoned a cab, and as he drove off cast one misty glance at the brass plate on the door. It was Andrew Ledwhistle's last day at the firm he had administered and nursed for 62 years of his life. There was a lump of emotion in the old man's throat as he stared out into the November night.

'Demented old fool,' he admonished himself. 'Still, I'll miss the old job and shouting at old Steinhouse.' But at least he had the satisfaction of knowing it was not passing right out of his hands. Ernest will do his job well, he thought; he was a likely lad. But there was this Andromikey boy. He was brought back to earth with a jolt.

The coachman blew on his fingers vigorously and a mound of hot air drifted into the November night mist.

Old Ledwhistle paid him a penny and stood for a moment in contemplation as the cab wound down the road, the feet of the rangey horses striking keenly to his ears.

'You are getting old, Andrew,' he scolded, 'you're nothing but a sentimental old codger.'

He climbed the steps and twisted the key in the lock. It opened more quickly than he was used and he stumbled a little as he entered the hall. The family were in the parlour. Usually at this hour his daughters were in their beds, but they were up tonight to hear the situation of the firm when Andrew Ledwhistle retired.

He pulled back the red-plush curtain and opened the door. His wife, who was about 65 but still able, was seated in a chair busy with some sewing. Francis, the youngest boy, was resting his head on his knee looking at a large book of lions. He was a white-faced little fellow of 6 or thereabouts, and he already showed an aptitude for figures. His thick black hair fell in a stain over his calm brow. His sister Charlotte was on her stool next to Fanny, a plump plain girl of some 16 years. Jane, the oldest in the family, was a shy musical girl of five-and-twenty. Engaged at a small table with curvy legs sat Ernest, on which burnt an oil lamp.

The scene was so peaceful and homely that old Ledwhistle halted for an instant on the threshold. His wife, a cheerful woman, rose to her feet and meekly laid her soft cheek against his weathered one. Little Francis jumped around him in delight and pulled his side-whiskers. Ernest hurried forward and dragged off his boots. Andrew Ledwhistle looked old and frail, and his loving family fussed and petted him until he was comfortable.

'Well, my loves,' he said, 'it is settled, is it not? Ernest shall go into the firm to be in my place.'

'But, Mr Ledwhistle,' interposed his wife, 'what of Richard Andromikey's grandson? He is to go with Ernest?'

'Yes my dear.' Old Ledwhistle looked at a paper he had drawn from his pocket. It was a letter. 'This,' he said, 'is from Martin Andromikey, who wishes to partner with Ernest and build up the firm.'

Ernest leaned forward. 'What is he like, Papa?'

'I've never met him,' protested his father, 'but he is coming to the office tomorrow morning.' He turned to his wife and daughters and youngest son. 'And now, my dears, to bed. I wish to talk to Ernest. We will surely meet on the morrow with God's help.'

They kissed each other soundly and retired. Ernest and his father talked well into the night.

Chapter 2

We will leave now, dear readers, the bright Ledwhistle parlour and, like a bird, pass out into the November night. We will journey down to a wharf where the slimy Thames moves like some loathsome adder, and the houses huddle together in squalid patterns. Here the lamplight falls on wasted limbs and shaking hands. It lights up sin and filth while, all aware, the cruel river twists its reptile course.

In one miserable hovel we will linger. The lamplight shines into the broken panes and struggles manfully to press yellowly into the gloomy interior. On the narrow bed is a young man. The room is in a state. Shoes, socks and trousers lie on the bare floor. A few blankets are flung over the thin form. Over him stands another young fellow, who has a bright red-check coat, green breeches and a top-hat full of dust on his head. Observe, reader, what now takes place. Read more slowly, because this is the plot of the whole story of the Tragedy of Ernest Ledwhistle and Richard Soleway ...

The boy on the bed groaned. His skin was like wax flowers in a Victorian vase. The eyes, instead of being warm and kindling, as was their wont, were infused with a metallic glitter. At a glance one could see he was struggling with the fever.

The man in the check coat sat down on the bed. His teeth bit fiercely into his lip, and his eyes had stormy clouds swirling round their vision.

'And this,' he muttered, 'is what that damned doctor called unimportant.'

While stout aldermen swill their ale and talk of the ingratitude of the poor, while their gross wives whom nobody loves laden with costly jewels, pick with lecherous fingers their dainty food, this is allowed to exist, dear reader! And, mark you, people of England and Wales, this does happen in these Satanic years, when justice is sat upon by the strong body of Gold.

The man picked up a spoon and poured a little water down the waxy throat. The hot hands grasped convulsively with weakening fingers and sweating palms at the sordid coverlet.

'Richard,' the boy said faintly, 'dear Richard, I wish to ask you something.'

The man sank to his knees and supported the palpitating head.

'Richard,' the gasping breath came again, 'dear Richard, promise me, promise me you'll go to Andrew Ledwhistle's in the morning. You see, Richard, Ledwhistle's father was the partner of my grandfather. Grandfather entrusted into Richard Ledwhistle's care a certain amount of money for me. He, when he died' – here the boy seized Richard Soleway's hand had a fierce grip – 'entrusted it to his son Andrew. Andrew Ledwhistle cheated me. I know he did, I know.' He lay back panting on the pillowcase bed. 'He cheated me of something like £35,000. Do you hear, Dick? Do you hear?'

The boy's voice rose like a plume of smoke. Richard never took his eyes off his friend. 'Yes,' he whispered urgently. 'Yes.'

'By the merest fluke,' Martin Andromikey went on, 'by the merest fluke I got to know that he was leaving and that his son Ernest was to carry on. I wrote to him telling him who I was. He doesn't know that I know he cheated me. I suppose his conscience made him give me the partnership. I was going to do such a lot, Dick.' The boy's eyes gazed with black intensity.

13

'Dick, I was going to make him suffer as he made me. But, Richard, listen. I want you to go and see him tomorrow. Do you hear, do you understand? ...' The boy's words trailed off. 'What was I saying,' he muttered. 'Oh, tell me, Dick, quick – before it's too late, Dick.'

'You were saying I was to see this Ledwhistle tomorrow, Mart,' his friend answered soothingly.

'Yes, yes, of course,' cried Martin Andromikey. 'Go and see him, Dick. Say you are Martin Andromikey ... Make him suffer, Dick ... make him suffer.'

Richard's eyes dilated. 'You want me to impersonate you?' he asked incredulously.

'Dick, Dick.' His arm was seized in a crushing grip. 'Promise me you will make him suffer. Promise me that, promise me.' The veins in his forehead swelled and filled, while his eyes started from their sockets.

'All right, Martin, all right,' soothed Richard.

The boy forced his hand away with dreadful strength. 'Promise me, dear Dick, promise me.'

Richard Soleway stood up. 'Before God,' he said with direful quietness, 'before God, I, Richard Howard Soleway, swear by all I hold true to make Andrew Ledwhistle suffer, if suffering be his due.'

Martin fell back. 'Dick,' he whispered, 'dear Dick.' That was all.

There was silence for a while. Then the body on the bed stirred. 'Pray for me, Dick,' he said. 'Pray for me.'

Richard knelt beside the fever-racked boy and prayed with all the simple fervour of his soul. The boy smiled and shut his eyes.

When the first ribbon of the sun threaded between the hovel window and trailed lacklustrely on the floor, Richard eyed its transfusing glow with distrust. Though it was yet early, that same sun had no doubt pried into scenes of dismal horror and

14

human degradation. It would be better if there was eternal night, he thought. He gazed down at his friend with pity and with envy, and gently crossed the two poor hands on the weary breast. For Martin Andromikey was dead.

Chapter 3

Ernest waited impatiently in the little office. His father was in the outer room talking to Jacob Steinhouse. The young man paced up and down. There was a quill pen on the desk and he picked it up and scrawled the words 'Ernest Ledwhistle and Martin Andromikey'. It sounded important and he flushed with pride as he thought that all this was to be his and Martin Andromikey's.

There was a sudden commotion on the stairs. A voice was raised in anger, and a young man shot into the room.

Ernest got to his polished feet. Facing him was a ballistic young man in a brilliant red-check coat and tails. His brown hair lay flatly on his head and curled sleekly onto his neckcloth. His long legs were wrapped in green breeches, and he held in his hand a top-hat of doubtful age.

Old Ledwhistle came into the room. He turned to Westbury, the junior clerk, in alarm. 'Who is this?' he asked, his very beard quivering like wheat in wind.

'My name is Andromikey,' said Richard quietly.

Ernest gasped.

Old Ledwhistle started forward. 'My dear young friend,' he amended, 'I had no idea.' He went on, 'Pray, pardon me for my incivility, but for a moment I was at a loss.'

Richard said nothing as he mentally sized up the cause of Martin's death. He hardly looks like a man who would cheat his dearest friend's grandson, he mused.

Old Andrew took
up his favourite stance

He became aware that Ernest was endeavouring to shake his hand. He bowed and sat down at length.

Old Ledwhistle took up his favourite stance, his back to the grate, hands clenched behind his coat-tails. Richard crossed his legs and hung his hat nonchalantly on his protruding foot. Ernest stood very straight and grave at his side, his clean young face flushed and nervous. As his father talked to them he could not help but let his eyes wander constantly to the person in the chair. He could not avoid admiring the gay coat and the careless way in which Richard looked about him.

Old Ledwhistle was thinking too. 'Damned self-assured,' he muttered inside. 'Still, that's what the firm needs. Ernest's got plenty of backbone, but he needs leading.'

At the end of the morning he had explained to them every slightest intricacy and deed. He took them both home to lunch and introduced them to his family.

As he bowed over the hand of Jane, Richard Soleway's heart gave an uneasy lurch. Was Martin in his true senses when he had accused Andrew Ledwhistle of his debt? Or had the boy been labouring under misapprehensions brought on by his burning fever? Yet, when he thought of the boy's black eyes, and felt again the desperate grasp on his arm, he felt sure this was not so. If Andrew Ledwhistle had cheated him he certainly did not show it. His manner was calm and friendly, and it was with a feeling of regret that Richard left the pleasant household for his own.

As he walked home down the dingey streets where men, whose very clothes were foul with the stink of beer, slouched, he thought of his own life in contrast with Ernest's. His thoughts wandered back to ten years before when a boy of 12 had gazed in horror at the prone figure of his dead mother. He had no recollection of a father, and it was 13 years since he had glimpsed his step-brother, a greasy man of 37 or so. The yellow lamplight, as shallow and artificial as the inmates of the wharf, found no responsive glow in the surly Thames. As he passed a broken shop, a figure came out of the shadow.

'Hallo, Mr Richard,' a voice said.

Richard faltered, and then walked on. At the door of his hut he turned and found the stranger behind.

Richard lighted a candle and set it on the broken table.

'What do you want?' he said hoarsely, as he shut the door.

The man sat down quickly on the bed on which a short time before the bitter body of Martin Andromikey had lain. In the glaring candlelight Richard saw the face of the man he was going to hate for eternity. The eyes were the grey of sleet, not the grey of a sparrow's wing, the lips were thick and rich red blood coursed through them. His chin had a deep cleft down it. His face was crossed with furrows like a ploughed field, and the cracks were filled with dirt. He wore a brown coat with tails and breeches, no shirt, and a blue spotted neck-cloth.

'What would I be wanting now?' leered he.

Richard gritted his teeth. 'Get out,' he said slowly and clearly.

The man backed. 'All right, Mr Richard,' he whined.

When he had gone, Richard shuddered. That evil waterman knew who he was! He would interfere with his plan! He fell once more to wondering if Martin had been wrong, but dismissed the idea. He felt hungry. The lunch he had eaten earlier had stimulated his appetite. When he did not eat he did not feel hungry, but the thought of that mutton and sponge-pudding tormented his stomach.

He did not take his clothes off, but lay far into the night thinking of the years to come. As he mused so, the water lapping by the bank sucked him down into darkness.

If, readers, you had journeyed into Richard's soul that dark night you would have passed down two channels: one bitter and twisted, filled with an all-enveloping swamp of hatred against the man who had caused Martin Andromikey's death.

19

The other one would have been bitter too, but in the spaces there would be pictures of the effect the firm's ruin would have on Ernest, his musical sister, his small brother and his pretty young mother.

Finally, Richard fell into a sleep, in which evil forces dragged him down with hypnotic eyes into the ever-waiting Thames.

Chapter 4

Gasper Liverwick slouched down the back streets. He made his way through the many alleys, and finally reached Thames Street. Here the lamps were yellower, the public houses more frequent and the people more degraded.

If, dear readers, when you come to the words 'public houses' and see in your mind's eye the bleary eyes and wasted limbs of the men and women staggering from such places, their yellow-skulled babies mewling in the gutters, do not call a curse on the wretched mortals who so displease your thoughts! Rather, call a fervent curse on the nobles and bishops of our London, for not giving the poor support and, what is more, self-respect – for regarding the silken coats of their many horses with delight, and for ignoring the parchment skins of their fellow-humans breeding and dying and neither eating or living, from one end of the town to another. When a heart is sick, and a mind stunted without education or enlightenment, when bodies curve unhealthily and carry disease in a warped line from head to toe, it is surprising how a glass of ale or spirits fills the guts and brain-matter with explosive feelings of relief, temporary well-being and a kind of gaiety. That is why the poor drink. To them the public houses, with warm fires kept burning to tempt the passer-by, serve as vast communal homes. Little matter that even their small coins go once more to furnish the rich brewery-owners with finer clothes and bedding, with more silken horses to pull their ladies' carriages, with more power to extract rents, taxes and tolls.

In such a home Gasper Liverwick sought refreshment. Sitting on one of the stools, sipping bad brandy, he waited for a friend. Round about on the benches ugly-looking sailors from the waterfront sprawled, and filled the air with brutal jests. Gasper smiled at the rude remarks and jeered in approval when one big brute swung the woman at his side out of the door by her hair. Blue-smoked air filled the room, and Gasper leaned back and waited and picked his teeth, which were very bad. Half an hour passed and the door swung back and a man slapped his shoulder, and called loudly for a jug of beer.

Rupert Bigarstaff was a man of about 36 years. His eyes were blue and twinkling, his features regular and pleasant, the cloth on his back of good quality. He was an odd fellow, known the length of the waterfront as the cruellest of men. He would not hesitate in doing the foulest murder, or torturing a reeling drunkard, but at the sight of a dog in pain, or a bird with a broken wing, his eyes would fill, and his hands grow as healing as the Apostles'. Many a person swore that he had the gift of healing, but he was feared for this the length of the water world. Some of his more personal acquaintances said he held the rich spellbound outside St Paul's of a Sunday. True, Rupert Bigarstaff was a strange man.

The two of them talked in low voices.

'It's getting hotter,' hissed Gasper Liverwick. 'I went to his place tonight and told him I knew, more or less.'

'He's out for Andromikey's money,' said Bigarstaff, and his face grew contorted. 'But he won't keep it long, will he, Gasper?'

His friend laughed, and such was the nature of it that the sailors on the benches stopped jesting, arms hung lifelessly round the narrow shoulders of their wenches. One man, with a big nose and a beautiful cloud of sunny hair that made him look lost beneath it, slapped his thigh and swore.

Rupert shot him a flashing glance and whispered in Gasper's ear, 'He overheard something, Gasper, me friend. Observe the way his fingers twitch.'

As Gasper could not fathom how twitching fingers denoted a person overhearing things that were not desirous to both parties, he did not trouble himself, but answered in an undertone, 'What do we do then, matey?'

'Leave it to me,' said Rupert, getting to his feet.

The yellow-locked waterman had gone out a moment before. They strode out into the night. A slight drizzle met them, and they watched their quarry turn the collar of his pea-jacket up about his ears. They followed him through the main streets and mean ones until, coming out of an alley, they saw him descend the steps of the wharf bank. He stood before turning onto his barge, maybe looking up through the drizzle and the fog, to where he dimly thought, as a child, stars had been. Then Rupert moved. There was a soft noise and down went the yellow head into the abyss of the deep. He came up and struck out for the bank. As his fingers grasped at the parapet Rubert brought his shoe down sharply on the bones. There was a screech from the man and he sank, the head now dark with water. Again, and for the last time, the clinging hands were stamped to pulp, and the body slid relentlessly away.

'Must we use violence?' asked Gasper, as they made their way homeward.

The friend at his side spoke in a soft crooning voice, the voice of a fanatic. 'That was not violence, Gasper Liverwick, that was tidiness. No man is worth human kindness. They're all soft relenting flesh, spineless. But in the next world there'll be a special kind of hell. Their bones will stretch the skin and be like iron. They'll scream for all eternity.' He laughed, and it was a nice laugh – the laugh of a schoolboy.

Gasper withdrew into himself and did not speak.

'We have one more call,' said Rupert finally. 'My very good friend Richard Soleway will be very glad to see us, and no doubt make us welcome.'

They came to the place where the said Richard lived, and Gasper peered through the window.

'There's no candle burning,' he said softly, 'but the lamp's shining on his bed. He's asleep – but fitfully, I should think, by the tossing of his body.'

Rupert flung open the door and shut it carefully behind them.

Richard sat up with a cry. His hands fumbled with the candle, and he bit his lip when he saw his unwelcome visitor again. He could not help but start at the face of the man next to him. It was lit with a bright light from within, and it glowed through the skin and teeth of Rupert Bigarstaff.

'What do you want?' he asked faintly.

'Nothing, nothing,' soothed Rupert, and such was his badness that Richard did feel soothed for the second.

'We want you to be our friend,' continued Rupert gravely. 'But I think it would not be in the nature of friendship to keep you from your rest, so I will say goodnight.' The glowing eyes lingered on his face. 'Sleep well, my dear young friend, and dream sweetly.'

When they had gone Richard lay shivering on his crumpled bed. He stumbled up at last and poured himself a glass of cheap whisky. He swilled it down and felt better, but he could not sleep. A thousand fears assailed him, fiery demons with sharp-pointed darts of hate attacked as he lay, his hand a-shaking on the coverlet.

At last, worn out with fear and wrestling inwardly with a foe that would not be suppressed, his head sank onto his breast, and he slept the sleep of the uneasy.

Chapter 5

Old Andrew Ledwhistle settled himself comfortably in his chair and brought out his diary. Old Andrew's diary was a kind of spiritual ritual with him; it was to him as water is to ducks. He opened it at March 9th, Saturday, the year 1851. His quill pen scrawled rapidly into the margin.

Met Father's partner's grandson today. He looks an intelligent youngster.

Here the pen pawed the empty air. Old Andrew leaned back and turned the pages slowly. November 11, 1783. He read slowly, as if savouring every word.

Father told me today that I was to be his successor in the firm. Am delighted. Am to partner with Peter Andromikey, whom I like greatly already. He is 13.

Old Andrew smiled and turned the pages rapidly.

April 4th, 1811. Father gave his blessing to Ruby and me.

His finger stopped at one page and, as he read the first lines, his head lifted and his eyes grew dreamy. 'Owing to Peter's death,' he heard his father saying, 'I am going to tell you the secret he entrusted to me. Richard Andromikey left to his grandson the sum of £45,000 in his will. He made one condition, however. Peter was not to give it to Martin unless he entered into the firm with your son and made good.' Andrew frowned. His father had sounded very solemn; it was just after the death of Ruby, he remembered. He turned over. One page read:

Father died tonight. Received a letter from Martin Andromikey asking me once more to lend him money.

He turned nearer to the back of the book.

Am to be married next week.

Then he returned to 1851 entry again. 'Martin seems very embittered but he is a good lad or seemingly is,' he wrote firmly. He then closed his big diary, shut it in his desk and shut his eyes.

Little did Old Andrew know that Martin Andromikey had found out about his money and that he was ignorant of the conditions. Little did he know that Martin was really dead, and had died with a curse on his lips which was directed against him. Little did he know that Richard Soleway was to be the instrument that was to break his heart. Little did he know that Francis was to end his days as a petty thief and that Ernest was to be ruined.

At that moment Ernest came into the room and, on seeing his father so preoccupied, tiptoed cautiously up to him and kissed the withered old forehead so marked by time. Old Andrew started. He laid his hand on his son's head and seated him on the stool on which his younger sisters often did their sewing.

'Well, Ernest,' he said softly. 'Are you happy?'

Ernest flushed. 'Papa,' he said painfully, 'I have something I would wish you to help me about. That is, the fact of the matter is, sir, I have been strongly attracted to the daughter of your friend Rubin Mansall.'

The father smiled.

'Go on, Ernest,' he bade.

'Well, Papa, that's all I have to say – except that I venture to guess Anna loves me too.' On the word 'loves' the young man coloured hotly and swept his hair from his forehead with a 'now it's over' gesture.

Old Andrew could not suppress a smile. 'But Ernest, you are but a little over 20.'

'I have a good job now, sir, and can well keep Anna in the comfort she is used to,' protested his son.

Andrew leaned forward. 'Let us wait till you are both older and more wise,' he said carefully. 'Anna is little more than a girl and you no more than a boy. Let me talk to your mother about it.'

'I am sure it must be love, Papa,' he said plaintively, 'for it hurts here,' and he laid his hand upon his heart.

This time Old Andrew laughed, without restraint. When his son had left him he lay with his feet on the fender and closed his eyes. The fire's ruddy colour made his eyeballs burn. He had not betrayed his displeasure when Ernest had told him of his love for Anna Mansall. He had nothing against Anna herself: she was a sweet girl, and a pretty one. But her father was another matter. Rubin had, at the death of Peter Andromikey, gone into the business with him. All had gone well for a matter of 18 years, till quite by chance Andrew had discovered he was systematically robbing his firm every year. On the pretence of retiring – for Old Ledwhistle liked and respected Mansall's wife – Rubin had been dismissed and the partnership dissolved. If indeed Ernest did have any real affection for the girl and one day wished to make her his wife, things would grow very awkward. No, Old Ledwhistle told himself, Anna shall never marry my boy. It will only bring unhappiness to both of them. Then he thought of Ruby Clacy whom he had married in 1811, and of the age he had been at the time. 'Yes,' he thought chuckling, 'I've been very lucky in marriage. Ruby was a good woman, and so is Mary.'

He rose to his feet, took the candles from the mantelpiece and pulled up the blind. Down Terence Street a cab moved, the cabby sitting like a sentinel on top. Below, in the house opposite, he could see Rachel Molson and her husband sitting before their fire, with the grey cat on the latter's knee.

'Jonathan Molson was always a fool about cats,' he mumbled, as he pulled the blind into place again.

Chapter 6

Richard sat on his high chair, his partner Ernest opposite him. The latter was diligently working. Jacob Steinhouse and Westbury were poring over a bundle of dry-looking deeds. The three looked so solemn and owl-like, especially Jacob Steinhouse, with his big eyes and quivering side-whiskers, that Richard wondered if he dared cough. He cleared his throat loudly. Three heads and three pairs of eyes were raised. Ernest's showed veiled approval, Westbury's irritated alarm, and Jacob Steinhouse's plainly told Richard what they thought of him. Immediately the heads were lowered. Richard wondered what would happen if he started whistling. He did so, and the scandalised eyes of Steinhouse leapt to meet him.

Richard got to his feet, yawned and said loudly, 'Coming for a drink, Ernest?'

Westbury gasped audibly.

Before the horror-stricken eyes of the two clerks, Richard walked out, his hand on Ernest's arm.

'I say,' said Ernest breathlessly, 'I've forgotten my hat.'

'You don't need one,' replied his friend.

'But I do, Martin, I do,' gasped Ernest, in distress as he was hurried along Talcorth Road. 'Where are we going?' he added, a note of interest creeping into his voice.

'To Comrades Street,' answered Richard with impatience.

'But Martin,' said Ernest in a whisper, 'that road consists mostly of gin-shops and opium palaces.'

'My dear Ernest,' said Richard, highly amused, 'it's plain to me you've led a very sheltered life. When one goes out for a drink, the right place to go is Comrades Street.'

In silence they entered one such shop. The young were absent, working their backs off them, for a paltry pittance. But the old were there – men and women whose very age made them indecent. Life held no more for them but gin and gin. The eyes were lifeless, their skin purple, their brains senile.

The two young partners made a queer contrast. Richard with his gay clothes looked more at home, but Ernest in his sombre black suit and high collar, his very face pink with embarrassment, looked strange, like a daffodil against a warehouse building.

Ernest shuddered. 'Why are these people allowed to mix with others?' he whispered in Richard's ear.

Any other time his friend would have grown heated and violent, but now he answered without passion. 'Because there are no graves for them to lie in.'

Ernest was silent for a space, but when an old man with looped and yellow-flecked eyes mouthed horribly and spat at him, he grasped Richard's arm and said, 'For God's sake, Martin, let's go back to the office. I can't stand this.'

So they went.

When they were once more seated at their desks, Richard began thinking over the plan that was to ruin the firm of Andromikey and Ledwhistle. Ledwhistle, he had found out, invested money on the Stock Exchange. He was a good and shrewd investor, and held many shares. Richard meant to bankrupt the firm, but he must have money to do it. He did not know how long it would take him to do what he planned, but on his solemn oath he knew he had given his promise to a dying man.

As the day finished and the time came to leave the books and manuscripts for another day, Richard's heart grew heavy.

He was unwittingly beginning to enjoy life for the first time. He said good-bye to Ernest and travelled into Billingsgate market. It had not yet closed and the scene was glaring and humorous. A man was sitting on a tub by a stall drawing. He alternately told the crowd of the excellence of his fish, and then drew them to the delight of the people, swimming in their natural element. Farther away another woman in a bright fringed shawl sold haddock while blessing all and sundry. Over everything hung the smell of fish. A salty, cold, icy smell one minute and a fierce, sickly one the next. There were all kinds of fish to be had. Big ones, little ones, round ones, flat ones, fish with spots on fish with stripes, some fish with rings, and just fish. The laughter of humour was everywhere. Here was the lighter side of life; here at least men were equal.

The night was early and Richard did not feel disposed to go to his bed. So he wandered round. At London Street, he stopped suddenly. Two men were fighting. One was tall and lithe, one thin and short. Richard would have passed if the desperate face of the short one had not been raised in earnest pleading towards him. The tall man was a rough-looking fellow, with ugly eyes and large hands. They were very out of proportion with his body, which was trim and wiry. He hit out harshly with one flabby fist, and the white-faced victim had his chin jerked back with a crack.

Richard stepped forward quickly. 'Heh,' he said impetuously, 'stop this.' He turned to the big-handed fighter. 'Your opponent's hungry, he's starving.'

The man grinned stupidly. 'I'm not exactly overfed meself.'

The white-faced youngster hung onto his arm. Richard pulled a couple of shillings out of his pocket and handed it to the man who had last spoken. He moved away, his hand on the other lad's elbow.

'Give us a few bob, mate, please,' the boy whispered.

'You need a meal first,' answered Richard, piloting his

acquaintance into a bar.

Silently the youth followed him to the parlour at the back. Richard ordered a toureen of thick soup and a plate of chipped potatoes and beef. To add to its completion, a mug of warm ale was set down.

The boy ate ravenously, never looking at his benefactor once.

Richard watched him cautiously. His eyes noted the sunken cheeks, the bright eyes and the threadbare clothes. Afterwards as the boy leaned back in the oaken bench, he ventured to ask him his name.

'It's Robert,' was the reply that came in faint accents, 'Robert Straffordson.'

Richard forbore to ask him any more questions. He took him that night to his hut and gave him a few blankets.

The boy did not thank him, but several times he saw the glittering eyes rest on his countenance.

When the morning came, Robert Straffordson had gone. With him had gone the first £5 note Richard had ever received. Richard did not feel vexed: he felt as if life was hopeless. Everything was so bitter and twisted. Little did he know what part Robert Straffordson was to play in the drama of his life.

Chapter 7

Sir Phillip Hobart, Chairman of the London Stock Exchange, was a thin, prominently-nosed man of about 58 or so. He had risen to the top of his ladder by sheer hard work, but not a little dishonesty. He was a man who was well pleased with life, but he was known to keep very much to himself. Not even his greatest friends knew of the old background of Phillip Hobart. He had no relatives, or seemingly not: if he did, he never visited them. As he walked briskly down Piccadilly and passed the Strand, many people stopped and bowed to him. Many a young society lad would gaze enviously after the prosperous knight.

Richard, it so happened, was walking in the opposite direction of that gentleman. He turned a corner. There was an angry shout and Richard saw Hobart sprawled on the ground, his hand to his head. A drab-coated youth was running in the direction he had just come from.

Richard raced in pursuit. He soon outran his quarry and grasped him by the collar. As his prisoner turned, he came face to face with Robert Straffordson. Richard felt himself go limp. By this time Phillip Hobart had reached them and quite a crowd had gathered. A withered constable came up to them in haste. Hobart stated his case and a charge was drawn up against the youth. Richard refrained from making any statement: he felt only pity for the degenerate boy beside him. He became aware that the group of people had been dispelled and found his hand being shaken by Hobart.

'I can never thank you enough, young sir,' he was told, while a pair of glowing grey eyes searched his countenance. 'If you are ever in need of help, come to me.' A card was thrust into his hand, and the knight walked off.

Richard looked at the card blankly. 'Sir Phillip Hobart, Knight. 'The Garrat', Bayswater, London.' Sir Phillip Hobart? Richard's mind revolved round and round. Surely – yes, it must be. He was the present Chairman of the Stock Exchange. Fate had introduced him to the very man he wished to know. He could have laughed, if not that the eddying mass of people were moving by. A horse-drawn bus passed him, and he saw his partner, Ernest. Ernest glimpsed him and waved his hand. He clambered aboard and climbed the stairs to the open roof.

As he was talking to the young Ledwhistle, Richard dropped the card that Hobart had presented him.

'I say,' said Ernest eagerly, 'do you know Sir Phillip?'

'Well, I had the honour of doing him some slight service a minute ago,' replied Richard. 'Do you?'

'Well, I don't myself,' volunteered Ernest, 'but he and Papa hate each other, I know. Father accused him of being dishonest one time when he had just been appointed, and they never speak nowadays.'

Ah, thought Richard. So Phillip and Old Andrew dislike each other, do they? Nothing could be better. I must further my acquaintance with Sir Phillip. Richard Soleway was one step on his way on the tragedy staircase of Andrew Ledwhistle and, though he did not know it, one step further to his own ruin.

Chapter 8

Anna Mansall sat demurely in the sitting-room awaiting the arrival of her lover, Ernest Ledwhistle. She was a striking girl of some 18 years of age, with thick black hair which rested in a loose coil on the nape of her neck. Her eyes were grey and set wide apart, her nose long and straight, her mouth large and generous. She was not beautiful in the accepted sense of the word, but she was arresting and pretty. She wore a gown of soft blue, and it was becomingly edged with lace.

The door opened and Eliza, the maid, entered bearing a tray. 'Master Ernest is here, Miss Anna,' she told her mistress. 'Shall I show him in?'

Anna nodded her assent, as she busied herself setting the cups out.

A moment later Ernest hurried into the room. 'Anna, my dearest,' he said as he touched her hand with his lips. He would have drawn her into his arms if Anna had not put her fingers to his mouth in urgency.

'No, Ernest, not now. Listen. I hear Mama on the stairs.'

Ernest sat down quickly in the chair opposite his love, and began making polite conversation.

He was rewarded for his prudence, for the door opened and Mrs Mansall entered the room. She was a stout woman in her late fifties. She was arrayed in an elaborate silk cap and a large quantity of petticoats. Her eyes were all but lost in a swelling of very red flesh, and what was glimpsed of them was unremarkable. Her mouth was thin and bloodless, her nose short and squat, wide and flared at the nostrils.

'My dear Ernest,' she fluttered, as she held out her hand. The flesh here too bulged round the rings and Ernest nerved himself as he bent over it. 'I hope you will be present at the ball I am giving for dear Anna's 19th birthday,' she said coyly. 'And I hear that your partner Martin Andromikey is in town.'

'Yes, Ma'm,' answered Ernest dutifully.

'Then we shall be delighted to invite him as well, shan't we, Anna dear?'

'Oh yes, Mama,' answered Anna. She tried to convey to Ernest that she would try and get her mother out of the room for an instant.

'Mama,' she said a minute later, 'will you entertain Ernest while I lie down? I don't feel well.' Before her mother could reply she darted out of the room.

'Oh dear, oh dear,' cried Mrs Mansall. 'Excuse me, won't you Ernest. I must look after the dear child.' And, still calling out 'Oh dear, oh dear,' she closed the door.

Hardly had Ernest sat down than the door opened and Anna darted in.

'She's chasing my ghost right to the top of the house,' she laughed merrily.

This time there was no staying Ernest. He seized her, and his lips found hers.

They were thus occupied – and a very good occupation I say – when Mrs Mansall came upon them.

'Oh, dearie me,' she wailed. 'Anna, my only child.' She sat down quickly and turned to the scarlet-complexioned Ernest. 'You, you scoundrel, Ernest Ledwhistle, putting this shock to me.'

Both Anna and Ernest looked in concentration at each other. 'You don't mind, Mama?' said Anna at length.

'Mind, my loves?' cried her mother. 'Love will find a way,

you know. When will you be married? Of course, I shall have to get Papa to talk to Ernest's.' She gabbled on, almost incoherently.

Ernest could have jumped with joy. He turned to Anna. 'Come back with me now dearest, and see Mama. I know she'll love you.'

'And I shall come too,' fussed Mrs Mansall. 'I'll just get my bonnet. Oh, but my only daughter, my darling little girl. But I must remember, I have not lost her, I have gained a son.' She could be heard reasoning in the hall outside.

Anna squeezed Ernest's arm. 'Dear Mama,' she said softly 'and dear Ernest.'

This gave dear Ernest a chance to prove how dear he was and they were only brought to earth by a discreet and forced cough by Mrs Mansall, who looked more ludicrous than ever in an enormous flowered bonnet.

A cab drove them all to Andrew Ledwhistle's and as they climbed out, the first realisation of what he had really done swept over Ernest. He remembered how his father had looked upon it rather lightly and seemed to consider him but a boy. As he led them to his mother he felt braver. They can't help liking her though, he reasoned. And besides it was his life.

The family were having afternoon tea.

'My dear Claire,' cried Mrs Ledwhistle affectionately as she kissed her old friend on the cheek, 'I haven't seen you for years. How are you? And, my dear, how Anna has grown!'

Andrew looked up from his old partner's wife's hand, and caught his son's eye.

Ernest slipped forward. 'Papa,' he said, and stopped.

'Yes, Ernest,' replied his father. 'Go on.'

Ernest began to flounder.

'The dear boy's shy,' cried Mrs Mansall in ecstasy. 'You see, Andrew, he loves my daughter as much as Anna loves him.'

Mary Ledwhistle gave an exclamation. 'Ernest,' she cried, 'I never knew! You knew told me!'

'I didn't know myself till but a week ago, Mama,' her son proffered. 'I told Papa and he said you and he would talk it over. But I do love her, Father,' he faltered lamely.

Old Ledwhistle's heart was heavy. 'Don't you think you're all a trifle hasty?' he said calmly.

Mrs Mansall's cup was suspended in the air. 'Andrew, don't you approve of the match?'

'Excellent, excellent, Claire,' responded Old Ledwhistle, 'but we must remember they're but children and not of age. They've got years ahead of them. Why, Ernest may think he's in love. I do not wish to hurt you, Anna my dear –' this in an aside – 'but it may be an infatuation you have for each other.'

'Papa, it isn't,' reproached Ernest. 'It is not, truly. I love Anna as truly as ever I'll love anyone.'

'There, you see,' cried his mother. 'It's all settled.'

Mrs Mansall could not restrain her delight.

'It is not all settled, Mary,' cried Andrew. 'Ernest is not going to marry Anna – or at least, not yet.'

Mrs Mansall was not daunted. 'Rubin will be calling on you shortly, Andrew,' she said, 'and everything will be settled up quite simply, with satisfaction to both parties.'

She bestowed a warm kiss on Mrs Ledwhistle and her daughters, nearly smothered little Francis in her voluminous petticoats, and swept out, Anna trailing dejectedly behind.

When they had gone, Ernest turned to his father in real anger.

'Papa,' he cried, 'I'm not a child. I love Anna, do you hear?'

'Yes, my boy, I do and I'm very distressed,' answered Old Ledwhistle sorrowfully. He turned to his daughter Jane. He addressed his eldest, 'Take your brother to the nursery, and Fanny and Charlotte go too.'

When they had gone, he bade his wife and Ernest be seated.

'Now,' he said worriedly, 'I will tell you a story. Many years ago, just after I made Ruby my first wife, Peter died. Then Rubin Mansall became my partner. 18 years later I learned he was robbing the firm. The partnership was dissolved. His wife and child are ignorant of his shame. And they must never know.'

'But what difference does that make?' cried Ernest impetuously. 'They won't know because I marry Anna.'

His mother, however, thought differently. 'You mean, Andrew, that Rubin has never forgiven you and never will?'

'Yes, my dear,' answered Andrew heavily. 'He would never consent to your marriage. It would make us all miserable.'

'But, Father,' cried Ernest wretchedly, 'it'll ruin my life. She's everything to me.'

'In that case, my boy – you cherish her happiness do you not?'

'Oh yes, Father, yes,' answered his distressed son.

'Well then,' reasoned his father. 'Do you love me, Ernest?'

'Papa,' cried Ernest, 'of course I do.'

'All right,' was the reply. 'Anna loves her father too, no doubt, and if she was ever to learn of his shame it would break her heart. Rubin would never agree to her marriage. And if you did get married without his consent, he would never forgive either you or her. Rubin is a determined man.'

'I see,' said Ernest blankly.

But he didn't. And Andrew knew that, but what he did not know was that Ernest loved Anna in a way which his father did not believe man could love woman. He did not know that the breaking off from Anna would bring about Ernest's downfall.

Chapter 9

Rupert Bigarstaff strolled up Ludgate Hill. His eyes stared straight ahead, but he saw nothing. 'I must do something about young Soleway,' his brain said. St Paul's glowed at the sky, its mighty dome a challenge to the unlovely things of the world.

'God was a fool to make a thing like that for the wretches,' he muttered.

He climbed the many steps and leaned against a pillar. He'd make 'em sit up tonight. He'd watch 'em writhe as they tried to stop their ears and couldn't. As a boy Rupert had been a queer little chap. He had a great memory for faces and astonished his wealthy parents by, at the age of 5, healing a dog who had been crushed under a carriage wheel. The family physicians had said it had been a miracle and he had been told to lay his hand on his dying father's poisoned hand. He did, but he didn't heal him. He had told his mother that his father wasn't fit for living. His mother had been frightened, he remembered. He'd been sent away to be home for abnormal boys.

A small group was already gathering round him. He had that gift. He instinctively attracted attention. They listened till the evening sun went that white red that warns the world his time has come. The trees waved dully, and still they listened. Finally, Rupert was silent. There was no clapping. There never was, for they one and all hated him and feared him.

She fell with hardly
a splash.

Rupert descended the steps and made his way homeward. He crossed London Bridge and rested for a moment on the rail. The sky was barred with red and gold. The eddying streams of colour raced over the water and were immersed in the shadows. It was very quiet, and when a footstep was heard on the cobbles he felt irritated. A young girl came towards him. Her face was streaked and dirty, her hair lank and black. Her eyes were large and without feeling, but the hand that clutched the fringed shawl was trembling. The girl said nothing. Her eyes rested hypnotically on the water. She stretched out her hand. She turned her head slowly to his.

'Do you think it'll be very cold and painful?' she asked, and her voice came from far away.

'Oh no,' answered Rupert. 'It won't. Shall I push you?'

'Oh no, no. I want to have the satisfaction of having felt courageous when I'm falling,' she replied, her eyes once more turned to the water.

She leaned over, and Rupert gave a sharp jerk.

She fell with hardly a splash. The water rippled and circled. Then all was still again.

Rupert felt pleased he had cheated her at the very end. Maybe, dear readers, you feel only horror at the thought of a young girl wishing to drown herself. But many a girl and many a boy have crept to find rest in the secretive waters of the Thames these many years.

Rupert turned and found Gasper Liverwick at his elbow. 'Hallo,' he said. 'Where are you going?'

'Wherever *you* are,' answered his crony, and arm in arm they journeyed to the waterfront.

Rupert entered his hovel and lit his lamp. It flickered strangely, not unlike the gleam in its owner's eye.

'Are we going to revisit Soleway tonight?' asked Gasper.

'No, I think not.' Rupert was final. 'We are to talk about him, though. Here, my friend, sit down.'

They sat down, and Rupert placed a bottle of stout on the table.

'Listen hard, Gasper,' he said, 'Richard Soleway today met Sir Phillip Hobart, Chairman of the Stock Exchange. Don't ask me how I know – I just do. About what he talked about I don't know, but I can guess. Andrew Ledwhistle, as we know, invests in the Stock Exchange. Probably our young friend wishes to get to know Sir Hobart for his own ends. That will mean success for the firm, and Richard Soleway will doubtless receive his money. Then we'll take a hand, Gasper, me friend.'

Gasper nodded his head in agreement. He wondered to himself what foul death Rupert would devise for Richard Soleway. Where would it all end?

Chapter 10

The streets of London were festooned with flags and bunting. The children, scrubbed and shining with soap and excitement and dressed in their patchy best, waited in a fever of impatience. The grown-ups too were giving sheepish smiles, for today was to be the day that Victor Radenstone – the name which conjured passionate acclaim from many men – was going to the reception at the Town Hall in honour of his great work in the Chinese Opium War. It was to be a public holiday as well, and there was to be beer and buns for the poor, presented by the charity of the Great Man himself.

There was a sound of horses' hoofs, and the crowds lining the narrow streets gave a lusty cheer – perhaps it was aided by the thought of free ale. A shining black carriage came into view led by a team of high-mettled horses, their nostrils dilated, their magnificent shoulders rippling under their satiny coats.

As the carriage swept by, Robert Straffordson gave a grim smile. He wondered what his prosperous step-father would say when he presented himself. In short steps, his shoulders bent, he made his way to the hall. Round at a rear entrance he was accosted by an officious individual. He was forcefully ejected and, his eyes smouldering, he skulked round the back. Here he was fortunate. A window, partly shuttered, afforded him entry. As he landed with a slight noise on the floor below him, he saw he was in a cloakroom. His hand stole into the nearest pocket, and out came a pair of satin gloves, a slightly soiled handkerchief and a knife. Robert stuffed them in his coat and opened the door a space.

The hall was full to the maximum. By a table sat a row of important, stomached aldermen. Opposite them sat their wives, and standing by the table was his step-father. The face was turned sideways and Robert saw the great Victor Radenstone's profile. No, he had not altered with the years. His body was large and muscular, and his hands strong and brown. But his face was the face of a city clerk. The nose was thin and wavery, the lips fine and sensual. The eyes were a watery blue, and they held the old familiar hunted look. Robert had inherited that expression. It was as if he was a timid dog hauling, rather doubtful of the consequences, on his leash.

Radenstone turned round slowly and for an instant his eyes met those of his step-son. There was no flame of recognition. He merely fixed his eyes on the people in the front rows. Victor, as he spoke in hackneyed phrases, was puzzled. The white and haunted face of the youth by the door had startled him not a little. Besides, had he not seen the same look in the mirror himself? Yes, those eyes were rather familiar.

He was brought back to earth by the sound of clapping. He gazed vaguely at the door again, but the boy had disappeared. He became aware that he was being led from the hall, and curious eyes feasted on him. There were the eyes – brown, green, grey-black eyes – but they all held the pinched, hunted look of the youth he had seen a minute ago.

Meanwhile Robert, after helping himself to a few pockets, wandered down the streets of the city. He loved his father with a love that was as fierce and heated as any. Years ago as a little boy he remembered how he used to get a feeling of warm contentment when he felt his small hand engulfed in that big one. He had not liked his mother, and until her second

45

marriage had stored his childish love up. When she had married Radenstone, he had showered all his affections on the big, weak-faced man. A film passed over his eyes. He had broken his father's heart 8 years ago when he had broken loose and left home. Gradually, year by year, he had fallen more and more deeply into the slough of thieving. He was nearing the water's edge, and as his eyes lighted on the dull grey of the water that moved sluggishly along he knew that he himself was growing like that year by year. Then Robert Straffordson laughed and was himself again.

Chapter 11

The spacious ballroom was glittering and mellow. The polished floor was an invitation to your feet, and made them want to slide, to ruffle the calm smugness of its surface. The orchestra, screened by tall ferns at the one end of the room, wafted forth a whirling melody. Here was colour, happiness and breathless beauty. The ladies' skirts and petticoats, brightly sequined, swished softly round their dainty feet. The many fans fluttered and revealed flushed and bright-eyed gaiety, while the men bowed over their partners' white fingers and dabbed hastily in their snuff boxes. Round the end of the floor on gilt-backed chairs, as stiff and upright as their occupants, rested the fond mamas who gossiped rapturously as they told each other 'how well dear Bertha and that young William Darcy looked together'.

Richard looked down at his pretty young partner, a vivacious girl with bewitching dimples in the velvet smoothness of her cheeks. By the door talking to Claire Mansall, was Rubin, her husband. He was a faded edition of his daughter, with black eyes and curved eyebrows. Rubin was looking angrily in the direction of Ernest, and his wife looked tearful and distressed.

As soon as the dance ended, Rubin strode up to Anna. He took her roughly by the arm. 'Is this how you repay me for my goodness, Anna? Where are your manners? As the hostess you must pay attention to your guests. Victor Radenstone wishes to have this next waltz.' But before the astonished girl could respond she was led off.

Ernest flushed furiously. Where had he heard that name before? Of course, he was *the* Victor Radenstone. He walked sulkily to a corner where his sister Fanny sat, her foolish face one bright beam.

'Come on Fanny,' said Ernest crossly, hauling her roughly to her feet, 'I wish you to dance this gavotte with me.'

Puffing, Fanny got to her feet. She was a silly girl with no beauty, and little brains. She irritated Ernest beyond measure by her empty expression and simpering ways.

Ernest looked moodily at Anna. She was pivoting lightly, her black eyes sparkling in the arms of a watery-eyed man. He felt he hated Victor Radenstone. Then he saw the kindly gaze in the man's eyes, and felt reassured.

He wished the dance would finish. The palms of Fanny's hands were wet, and short bursts of breath came from her clenched teeth. He tried to loosen her stubby fingers from his sleeve. He felt sure she would mark his new suit.

There was a final chord from the orchestra, and Richard walked over to him. He bowed briefly over Fanny's hand and escorted her gallantly to her wall-flower seat. With a guilty pretence of an excuse he left her, and went his way to his partner.

'I say Martin,' cried Ernest, 'this is awful. Look at Anna. It's scandalous.'

Richard smiled. 'She's just as upset as you,' he reassured.

Ernest kicked the door angrily. A moment later Anna swept over to them. Ernest hurried forward and took both her hands in his.

'Anna,' he said peevishly, 'how could you?'

Anna glanced reproachfully at him, under lowered lids. 'Papa does not approve of you, I feel sure. When will you approach him about our love for each other?' she asked him earnestly.

the youthful lovers waltzed
together and Mr Marvell
was furious.

Ernest's eyes clouded. 'I shall ask him tonight, dearest,' he resolved.

Anna turned to Richard. 'I hope the dancing is to your liking, Mr Andromikey,' she smiled.

'It would be much more enjoyable to me if you would honour me with the next dance,' replied Richard. He turned to Ernest. 'You do not object, partner?' he teased.

Ernest assented gaily this time. As he watched the two walk away, he became aware that a man was speaking.

'Excuse me, my dear young sir, but my name is Victor Radenstone.'

Ernest started. 'Not really?' he said. 'Indeed, this is a great honour, Sir.'

'The honour is entirely mine,' confessed Radenstone, bowing. 'I do hope you will not think me impertinent if I ask you when you and Miss Anna are to be betrothed. You see, during the dance the young lady was so flattering as to confide all to me. And my chivalry, though I blush to say it, has been aroused.'

Ernest looked downcast. 'Mr Mansall does not, I feel sure, approve of me, Sir.'

Victor Radenstone looked dreamy. 'That must be altered,' he said slowly. 'Tonight after the ball I will go with you and Miss Anna to his study. There we will persuade Mr Mansall that you are the best of fellows.' Ernest's eyes began to regain their sparkle.

'I can never thank you enough, Sir,' he stammered.

Radenstone cut him short. 'I have a son too,' he said. 'By marriage, but I have not seen him for years.'

Ernest hurried away to convey the good tidings to Anna. They both could hardly restrain themselves and were heartily glad when the guests began to disperse.

Finally, only two young men remained, besides the other three: Michael Standing, and a young nobleman named

Lionel Dante. These, with great difficulty and not a little tact on behalf of Anna, were coaxed to go home. Then Anna, Radenstone and Ernest made their way to Rubin Mansall.

Rubin Mansall was just reclining in his armchair, his glass of brandy beside him. Rubin was rather partial to a glass of warm spirits.

'Impudent young puppy,' he muttered savagely, as he crossed his feet on the fender. He was so sitting when his daughter and her two friends came softly into the room. Rubin was hardly civil to Ernest, and only barely polite to Radenstone.

Ernest began to fidget with his fingers. Radenstone broached the subject boldly. 'I have formed some affection for these two young people,' he said, 'and am well interested in their welfare.'

'Damned good of you,' barked Rubin, and Radenstone flushed darkly. 'Furthermore, Sir,' he continued, 'they wish to marry.'

As he spoke these last words Anna clutched her father's hands.

He threw her off roughly and turned on Ernest. 'Who do you think you are?' he said in a low voice. 'Why you, you little puppy, you are a partner in a firm that is as poor as it is dishonest.'

Ernest started forward, but Radenstone stayed him.

'I don't think that's quite fair, Mr Mansall,' he said grimly.

'As for you, you yellow-skinned, yellow-natured drug-curer, why don't you return to your heathland, and tame your crooning friends,' Mansall cried.

Radenstone kept his temper with difficulty. But Ernest could not. He sprang forward, his eyes glowing.

'If Father's firm is poor,' he stormed, 'it's because you stole all the money we ever got, and if we're dishonest it's because you ruined our name, and couldn't keep your hands to yourself.'

Rubin clenched his fists and grew purple in the face.

'What if I did steal your blasted money?' he screeched. 'The salary would never have kept me, or Anna or Claire, decent.'

Radenstone gripped Ernest's arm in alarm. 'Be quiet Ernest,' he cried. 'This is a great shock to Anna.' He was just in time to catch the young girl.

Ernest carried her over to the couch. 'Anna, my love,' he cried brokenly, 'forgive me, oh forgive me.'

Rubin towered above him. 'Get out,' he thundered, 'get out.'

Radenstone pulled Ernest to his feet as the door opened and Claire Mansall hurried in.

'Oh,' she cried hysterically. 'Anna, my love, what is it? Ernest, what do you wish here? Rubin, help me quick. Oh Anna, Anna.'

She bent down and, helped by her husband, carried their daughter out of the room.

Ernest almost ran after them but Rubin had taken his precaution. Cadenlike, his manservant, politely showed them the door.

There was nothing for it but to go. As Radenstone pushed his young charge into a cab, he heartily cursed himself for his own clumsiness.

Ernest was beside himself with grief. 'Father told me to be prudent,' he cried. 'Oh, what have I done to her? She will hate me.'

Radenstone tried to soothe him. At the door of the Ledwhistle house he paid the cabbie and helped the young man up the steps.

As soon as Ernest was over the threshold, helped by old Wishlock, he turned and disappeared down the street. 'Fool that I am,' he groaned. 'Oh Robert, Robert, where are you?'

Chapter 12

Richard faced old Steinhouse with a cold smile.

'I know that I am young and foolhardy,' he said, 'but I also know that you are old and behind the times. These sums you invest in the Stock Exchange are too small to be of any profit to us. All I have done is to invest £700 in shares. When the shares go up, you will see whether I am prudent or not.'

Old Steinhouse was silent. He knew it was no use arguing with this young devil. He was too go-ahead, too reckless. If anything were to happen – he shuddered at the thought.

Back in the office which he shared with his partner, Richard took Ernest by the shoulder. Ernest's raised face was completely devoid of colour.

'Ernest,' said Richard gently, 'you can't go on like this. You'll be ill.'

'I've not seen Anna since that day last week,' replied the young man in distress. 'I've written, but I received no reply. Oh Martin, I must see her, I must know.'

'All right,' said Richard, 'you shall know. I shall make a point of seeing Miss Anna and arranging for her to see you. If need be I shall bring her here.' He swung on his heel.

'Where are you going, Martin?' cried Ernest.

'To visit Miss Mansall,' replied his partner. 'I shan't be long.' He gave Ernest a reassuring smile. 'Don't worry. She loves you as much as ever, I'm sure.' And with this Ernest was well content.

Richard walked briskly down the street. He liked Ernest, and was sorry for him. He could afford to be good to the young man, he thought. For yesterday, much to Jacob Steinhouse's disturbance, he had invested a considerable amount of money in the ship *Pirate's Fancy*, which was bound for the West Indies. He was confident that the money would be trebled, and step by step he would invest more and more, till the crash came.

He rang the bell of Anna Mansall's house, and was admitted into the hall. Soon Anna joined him, and led him into the sitting-room.

'How is Ernest?' she begged him, as soon as they were out of earshot of the maidservant.

'He is very stricken,' replied Richard, 'for he thinks by revealing the truth about your father's – "retirement", shall we call it? – that you will never forgive him.'

'Oh, tell him I do, I do with all my heart,' cried Anna. 'I know he has written, but Papa took all the letters and burnt them privately.'

'When can you see him?' asked Richard. 'He is beside himself with remorse.'

'It is I that is beside myself with shame,' said Anna in a whisper. 'To think that Papa should rob dear Mr Ledwhistle and nearly ruin him.'

Richard patted her hand in sympathy. 'Does your mother know?'

'I fear she does,' Anna answered. 'She has never left her room for 3 days. I do believe Papa is being sorely punished.'

'Well, I must leave you now,' said Richard at length.

'When can I see Ernest?' cried his hostess wildly.

'You shall see him tomorrow,' resolved Richard. 'I shall call for you at 11 in the morning.'

Murmuring her thanks, Anna wished him good-bye and, with a lighter heart than the one she had carried for the past week, fled upstairs to the sanctity of her room and wept.

Meanwhile Richard was talking to Ernest.

'Oh Martin, Martin,' cried the young fellow, searching his friend's face with flashing eyes.

'The forgiveness, she says,' enlightened Richard, 'is entirely on her part. She is to come here tomorrow, and told me to assure you that her heart is yours for ever.'

Ernest sank back in his chair.

'Thank you,' he said, 'thank you, Martin.'

Chapter 13

It was a sunny morning when Anna Mansall hurried up the stairs, to fall into the arms of her lover. It was still the same bright morn when Old Ledwhistle climbed the same steps and found his old partner's daughter in his son's arms. His eyes twinkled as they drew apart.

'My dear Anna,' he said. 'Can you forgive me?'

'Oh, yes, yes,' cried Anna, 'a thousand times.'

'What of your mother?' asked Andrew as he placed his stick by the door.

'I am afraid she is very much humbled by my father's disgrace,' Anna sighed, 'and I think papa is being punished. He is quite cast down.'

While this conversation was going on Robert Straffordson followed his father down through the city. His eyes were thoughtful as he saw the broad shoulders and weak head before him. He quickened his footsteps. He wondered what he should do. Would Victor Radenstone be pleased to own him? In a way he doubted it.

As he crossed the road he saw a cab bearing down on his father. He flung himself on the burly figure. There was a shout, a hoarse cry from the cabman, and Robert saw the shining blackness of the horses' hooves before the ground rushed with sickening force towards him.

Chapter 14

Robert lay on the bed, his brow furrowing as the June sun sought his eyes. He was in a large room with warm gold fittings. The boy heard the sound of cabs' wheels in the road below. He lay there languid and looked at his hands. They were thin and white and veined. A bell was on a small table by the side of him. He picked it up and shook it, while his wrist bent with the weight.

At once the door opened and a woman came into the room. She wore a white apron, and from her stringed cap peeped a fuzzy grey curl. She smiled at him and felt his pulse.

Robert said nothing, but watched her drowsily. He watched her move to the door and heard her footsteps on the stairs. Then he heard other footsteps, strong ones, slightly loping. The door opened and Robert saw his father.

'Robert,' cried Radenstone. 'Oh Robert.' He fell forward and kissed his son.

Straffordson felt suddenly tired and happy. His hand was once more in that well-loved big one.

As he slept, his father wept. 'Robert,' he said over and over again. As he felt the thin fingers tighten their grasp on his he thanked the good God for his mercy. Yet was it really mercy? His son would never walk again, for his legs had been amputated.

He stayed there all through the day and when finally Robert awoke supported him with his arm.

'Father,' said Straffordson, 'I'm frightened. I keep feeling for my legs but they're not there. There's only spaces, Father. Oh, what has happened?'

Briefly, his throat threatening to choke his words, Radenstone related the accident.

'Robert nodded dumbly. He struggled a second, then lay back quite still.

'Don't leave me,' he said faintly. 'Don't ever leave me, Father.'

Then, as the shadows lengthened, they lay together, father and son, all barriers swept aside, and Robert slept.

All barriers
swept aside.

Chapter 15

Fanny Ledwhistle stared dully up at the young man who was picking up the parcel that had slipped from her short fingers. Her mother smiled brightly and thanked him profusely. He was an immensely tall and thin young man, with huge, black-rimmed spectacles and nervous blinking eyes. His mouth hung open, while his wrists protruded well below his coat sleeves.

'The pleasure is entirely mine, Ma'm,' he returned, and he spoke with a pronounced American accent.

Fanny wondered absentmindedly if his voice had broken yet, or was just in the stages of doing so. One minute it was cracked and boyish, next it was lost in the depths of bass manhood.

'My name's James Coney,' he volunteered.

'Oh, indeed,' replied Mrs Ledwhistle. 'Well, thank you once again. Good morning.'

Stammering and blinking alternately, Mr James Coney was dismissed and Mrs Ledwhistle swept on majestically. 'Well,' she said to Fanny, 'I've heard these foreigners are forward, but Mr Coney is beyond himself.'

Fanny said nothing. She was already in the stages of a great romance, in which Mr Coney, whose voice was by this time broken, rescued her gallantly from drowning.

'Fanny,' cried Mrs Ledwhistle irritably, 'I've spoken to you 3 times, what is the matter?'

At their house, Jane was busily playing the piano, and Fanny was quite lost in admiration at the way in which her sister's sensitive fingers lingered over the mellow keys. Old Andrew was leaning back in his usual armchair, beating time with his foot. As his wife took off her shawl and bonnet, he chuckled.

'Andrew,' said Mary, 'what is making you laugh?'

'Young Andromikey invested £700 in a ship bound for the West Indies about 3 months ago,' replied Old Andrew happily, as he took his wife's hand in his. 'And furthermore our money has been doubled, for the trip proved highly successful.'

'I am glad,' cried Mary smiling, 'for I know your heart and soul is in the firm.'

'My heart and soul belongs to you, my dear,' replied Old Andrew huskily. 'You and our fine girls and sons.'

'As you know, Andrew,' related Mary, 'Fanny dropped her parcel and a most peculiar young American picked it up. He seemed very taken with Fanny – hardly took his eyes off her the whole time. But he was very forward.'

Jane giggled, and Charlotte tried to control herself also.

Fanny flamed an ugly red and Mrs Ledwhistle wished she wasn't so plain and stout. Still, that young fellow had seemed more than usually attracted. Now if it had been Jane, she mused. She looked hard at the girl at the piano, at the auburn hair and slight figure. Now that would be sensible, but Fanny!

Old Andrew smiled at his wife's expression. 'Wondering where Ernest is?' he asked.

Mrs Ledwhistle shook her head. 'No, I know where he is already. Rubin invited him for lunch.'

Charlotte put her head on one side. 'You know, Papa, Uncle Rubin has altered a great deal. Why, before three or four months ago he hardly ever came here, or invited us there.'

Old Andrew winked slyly at his wife. 'Yes,' he said slowly, 'Rubin's changed, but for the best. Have you finished your embroidery yet for your brother's wedding? You have not much time, you know.'

Charlotte sighed. 'It's very strange,' she said, 'but the threads seem to knot and break. Whatever I do, I doubt if Anna will ever use it.'

Mary Ledwhistle laughed in agreement. 'Come along, Fanny,' she called. 'Come and take your outdoor attire off.'

Fanny dutifully followed her mother out into the hall.

'Mary,' Old Andrew's voice floated up to them, 'don't forget that the Mansalls and Victor Radenstone and his son are coming tonight to dine.'

'Oh,' cried Mrs Ledwhistle incredulously, 'I'd quite forgotten. Where on earth did I put the key to the linen cupboard?'

Jane sat all through the afternoon at her beloved piano. Many a time Old Andrew would look in wonder at her, for the notes that she played seemed to hang clean in the air, till they dropped tinkling and sparkling into the mind.

'Father,' asked Jane suddenly stopping her playing and laying her soft head on his knee. 'What do we say to poor Mr Straffordson?'

Old Andrew stroked her hair with gentle fingers as he puffed contentedly at his pipe. 'We just act as if nothing had happened,' he advised. 'You see, he is only young – little over 20 I should say – and like all young things he is very proud. Now do not worry your silky head, but pray for me.'

As the dreamy melodies once more waved about his ears Old Andrew thought sagely, yes, like all young things, he is very proud. So's young Andromikey. I'm worried about him. He's so aloof, as if he resented any charity on our part. When he is 27, I shall most certainly give him his money. I warrant I'll have to convince him of its legality before he'll take it. He chuckled quietly, and Jane on her stool smiled.

Later that evening they all sat 'round the fire – Rubin,

Radenstone and Old Andrew with glasses of good wine before them, and Robert and Ernest pulling rather self-consciously at their pipes. Robert was in a chair with a gay rug over his unsightly trunk. He was quite content with his lot. Later on, when he was stronger, he was to be fitted with two wooden legs. Mrs Mansall talked untiringly to her friend Mary Ledwhistle, while Jane sat quietly by her brother, her hands folded on her lap. Robert, whenever he looked at her, felt restful and tranquil. Once she looked at him, and found his eyes resting on her. She smiled, coloured and looked the other way. Radenstone kept close to him, for he did not wish ever to be away from his son again. Robert too liked him near, for Victor radiated protection and the love he craved.

Soon – ah, all too soon – the evening drew to its close, and the Radenstones and Mansalls bade them good-bye. Jane, as Robert bowed over her hands, felt more and more attracted to him. Then there was a slamming of doors, a crack of a whip, and he was gone.

Chapter 16

James Coney peered shortsightedly at the shop-window. He wondered if he could afford to buy that very important-looking hat. It would look so elegant, he mused. As he glanced up and down the street to see if anyone was watching him as he took out his wallet, he saw Fanny panting in his direction. He whistled softly, put his note-case hurriedly back, and bowed. Fanny was very taken aback when the very stranger who had been the central figure in her dreams for some time past accosted her. She blushed and gave a shy smile. James felt he had scored.

'Would you care to honour me by letting me walk a little way back with you?' he drawled.

'Well – I – er, that is –' gasped the flattered Fanny.

But her admirer had already taken her arm and was steering her across the street. 'You know, Miss, Miss –' Here James faltered affectedly.

'Ledwhistle,' interposed Fanny with more intelligence than was her wont.

'Miss Ledwhistle,' continued James, 'I couldn't get you out of my mind yesterday.'

Fanny felt as if she could cry, and nearly did when James added: 'I hope you don't think I am being a nuisance, but you see I got the instinctive feeling – I hope I do not presume – that you were drawn just the teeniest bit to me as well.' Here he

James had
already taken her
hand.

cast a shy glance at Fanny, who stared at him stupidly, her mouth hanging open.

'Oh yes, yes indeed, Mr Coney,' she gasped. 'That is – oh dear, what have I said?'

'My dear Miss Ledwhistle,' cried James, 'let me say I much admire you.'

Fanny did not know what to say.

When she was bidding James Coney goodbye later on, she was both flustered and breathless. What would her mother say about her meeting a young man like that, and freely admitting her love for him? But Mrs Ledwhistle, when Fanny confusedly told her, just laughed and said it was about time one of her daughters got married.

That night Richard came to dine, and Old Andrew congratulated him on his successful venture. 'But of course, Martin,' Old Andrew told him, 'you must not repeat your action. It's too reckless, you know.'

Ernest spoke slowly, from his seat by the table. 'I don't agree, Father,' he said. 'You were very pleased when all this money came in now, were you not?'

'But Ernest,' choked his father. 'You can't put the same sums into unsteady gambles for the rest of your days. Why, it would mean ruin.'

His son waved his hand in an impatient gesture. 'But Papa, life is one gamble itself. Everyone takes risks. At your age, Father, there's nothing left for you but to take risks.'

Old Andrew shook his head heatedly. 'You're wrong, boy,' he stuttered. 'Where do you think the firm would be today if I had gambled in my time? No, no, it's too dangerous, too unsteady.'

He cleared his throat testily, and Ernest was wise enough to hold his silence.

Richard, however, was not to be subdued. 'Sir,' he said distinctly, 'does not this firm belong now to Ernest and me?'

Old Andrew could not but guess the intrusion behind this bald fact. He coloured, and Ernest sprang angrily to his feet.

'How dare you, Martin,' he thundered. 'I think you'd better go.'

'Now, now,' soothed Old Andrew. 'He's right, you know, my boy – only my whole soul's wrapped up in the firm, and I can't quite realise I do not have a hand in its workings any longer.'

It was Richard's turn to colour. 'I'm sorry, Sir,' he said, quietly. 'You know best, but I do want to build up the name of the Ledwhistle and Andromikey.' And as he said this Richard felt more of a hypocrite than he should have done.

When the two young men had gone, Old Andrew sat awhile in his chair. Finally, he got up and crossed to the window. The larches surrounding the Moleson house swayed darkly, and all the street seemed shrouded in the dark and unending drift of sleep. The lamp-lighter had visited here long ago, and the yellow glow shone and swam in the gutter below. Up above, a crescent moon brightly rested among his blue-black train of clouds. A cruel wind was rising, and Old Andrew shivered slightly. Yes, he was getting old. His hand trembled as he turned away. Ah well, he couldn't complain. He'd lived his years, and if his maker saw fit to call him – why, he'd go willingly. He chuckled. He couldn't very well do anything else. He puffed at his pipe, and brought once more his diary out. He was glad the feud between him and Rubin had ended – better for all sides, he thought, as his pen scratched away. Ernest was to be married soon, and he and Mary were delighted. Anna was a good girl. Why, when Young Martin married he would give him his money and his blessing.

Old Andrew stopped writing and lifted his head. Martin ... ah Martin, that impetuous young rascal, how his thoughts seemed to dwell continually on him. The boy was so proud and so distant. He never unbended. He'd seemed to keep a barrier between himself and them. Only with Ernest did he seem to relax. The sonorous notes of the old clock boomed out and he hurriedly finished his entry. It was a matter of seconds only before the candles were extinguished and the diary locked away.

Chapter 17

'Why hasn't Old Ledwhistle thrown Richard out of the firm yet?' worried Rupert Bigarstaff. 'That last venture must have lost them a small fortune. I wager Old Ledwhistle was pretty soured by it.'

'And rightly so,' said Gasper Liverwick. 'The young beggar narrowly missed bankrupting them.'

Rupert nodded. 'Hm,' he assented ungraciously, 'but it's a damned nuisance. We could use some money, Gasper, me lad.'

He got to his feet, shoved the table away from him and they walked out into the street. The pavements were thronged with people hurrying hither and thither. Gasper suddenly clutched Rupert's arm.

'Look,' he gasped. 'If it isn't young Master Francis himself.'

'Well, well now,' breathed Bigarstaff. 'Now isn't this going to be jolly! He's a proper young gent.'

Little Francis Ledwhistle at the age of nine was skipping gaily along the sidewalk clutching to himself a large ledger. His thick curls were free and his eyes were glowing like small boys' eyes will do when they are for the first time out in the great world of the city, on their own.

'Come, Gasper,' cried Bigarstaff in a pleasant voice, 'I'm quite sure our little friend would love us to keep an eye on him.'

Uneasily Liverwick followed, his ugly face in a worried frown.

'What's the game, Rupert?' he asked as they paced after young Francis.

'Really,' answered his crony, mockingly. 'You're very crude. What possibly could be our game? Use your imagination,' he snapped curtly. 'Why on earth should the child be by himself in the city?'

The child passed down a dark alley and his hopping slowed into a subdued walk. For the first time he was a tiny bit frightened. It wasn't such fun after all slipping away from Fanny like that. He wondered tearfully why those two men were following him. He didn't like the way they gazed at him. Perhaps, perhaps ... In a trice little Francis was running.

The footsteps behind him became quicker too, till Gasper and Bigarstaff were on his very heels. Francis felt his heart in his throat. Then it was in his mouth as the long arm of Rupert snaked out and held him by his collar. He stood there panting and gasping, his breath coming in great thudding bursts.

'Well,' said Bigarstaff, 'that's a nice thing to do, running from your friends, me little dear.'

He bent down swiftly and dived his hand into the boy's pocket.

'Huh,' said Gasper as a minute handkerchief was brought to light, finely edged with lace. 'Quite a toff, ain't we?' he murmured, as he sniffed daintily.

The two of them roared with laughter and Francis snivelled. Rupert dealt him a mild cuff on the ear and he stuffed a trinket into his trouser pocket.

Then everything happened at once. There was a sound of light shoes on the cobbles and the two rascals took to their heels. James Coney picked the child up and dabbed helpfully at the boy's stained cheeks with an equally stained piece of cloth. 'There, there, my little boyo,' he soothed. When Francis had calmed down somewhat he asked the child its name.

'My name,' said little Francis proudly, 'is Ledwhistle.'

Little Francis took to his heels, ringlets flying.

'No, it can't be,' gasped his rescuer, frantically. 'Oh, this is fate.'

Francis found his hand seized in that of a large boney one, and found he was being trotted along at a great rate. His small legs went pattering after each other till, almost running, they reached his house.

'Oh, Master Francis,' squealed Connie, the parlour maid, 'how could you!'

They were ushered into the hall, and Francis was immediately enfolded to his mother's capacious bosom.

'Frankie, you wicked boy,' she sobbed and scolded.

James coughed.

'Good heavens,' cried Mrs Ledwhistle, 'is it – is it Mr Coney?'

'Yes, Ma'am,' replied that worthy modestly.

He was then swept into a large room, and here the family were assembled. Once more James was forgotten as in turn the returned one was petted and cooed over.

Then Andrew lurched to his feet. 'And to you, my dear young sir, I can but be ever indebted.'

He paused for words, and Francis began talking. 'But you don't know all, Papa,' he cried shrilly. 'Two wicked men accosted me and stole that lace handkerchief of mother's, beside that necklace I got when I was four.'

James waved his hand modestly. 'Oh, that was nothing, sonny,' he said wisely.

Old Andrew's eyes met those of his wife. They crinkled at the corners as he saw Fanny blushing a fearsome red. Charlotte bent suspiciously over her book.

Soon James was seated and accepted by all. His drawling voice, and blinking eyes, with his boyish hair on end, made him look rather pathetic. Fanny, as her eyes rested on his face, felt her heart give a silly leap.

In the fireside corner on the couch sat Anna. On her knee

sat a little boy in petticoats, for two years Ernest and she had
been happily married. But Old Andrew had aged. His hair was
scantier than before, while the few locks were white and
grizzled. His beard too was white, but here and there threaded
a thick black hair. It was the firm that had aged him, for since
Richard Soleway's unsuccessful investiture the business had
dropped to its minimum.

'You will stay to lunch, won't you?' invited Mrs Ledwhistle.

'Oh well,' said James, '– that is, if everybody's willing.'

He looked pointedly at Fanny, whose plain face was quite
intelligent with the love that glowed through her.

There were eager assents on all sides, and so James became
a firm friend of the Ledwhistles.

Chapter 18

Phillip Hobart, Knight, sat ponderingly at his desk. His long fingers drummed in irritating rhythm on the polished suface. Before him sat Richard Soleway.

'Look here, young fellow,' he advised. 'Don't you think you'd better turn your hand to something you understand? The Exchange isn't a gambling den, Dick.'

'I know what I'm doing,' rapped Richard. 'I wish to invest £2,800 in cash, and £5,000 worth in bonds in the New Westworth Papers.'

'But it's the most surest thing that that will fall through,' gasped Hobart.

'I have the cash here in notes,' continued Richard. 'I wish you to manage it for me at once, understand?'

He left a scandalised but resigned Chairman.

Chapter 19

Jacob Steinhouse came into the outer office, in breathless haste.

'Martin,' he gasped, 'Master Martin, what does it mean?'

'What does what mean, Steinhouse,' asked Richard tersely.

He turned to Ernest, who was gazing open-mouthed at the paper the old man had thrust on his desk.

Martin leant over and took it from him quickly. His heart gave a great leap as he read:

Westworth Paper fails to sell. The well-known firm of lawyers, Ledwhistle and Andromikey, lose over £7000.

He scanned the society gossip column and read:

For some time past it has been noticed that Young Andromikey has been making wild speculations. This, we have no doubt, will be his last venture.

Richard felt a wave of thankfulness sweep over him. He had accomplished his task: now he could go and lead his own life. The curse of Martin Andromikey had been fulfilled.

Ernest slumped forward. 'My God, Martin,' he screeched. 'You damn fool, you damn blasted fool!'

He got to his feet slobbering, while Old Jacob wrung his hands in agony. 'What will Old Mr Andrew say?' he moaned.

'It will break his heart. Oh, oh.' He sat down suddenly, and shakily mopped his brow.

Richard gave a weary smile. He got to his feet and swallowed.

Ernest grabbed his arm. 'No,' he cried shrilly. 'No, you're not going, you dirty crook. You'll get years for this.' He then lapsed into the boy he was again. 'Who's going to tell Father?' he groaned sickly. 'My God, who's going to tell him? He'll know now – and just think,' he said in a low voice. 'He's bound to see the papers.'

It was a rainy day in July, and the weather outside was roaring and whistling down the streets. Ernest looked out of the rain-blotted window and choked in a whisper: 'He's coming here!' He turned a white face to the group before him. 'We've got to stand by him,' he ordered tensely. He cast a withering glance at Richard. 'As for you,' he spat out. 'You mustn't leave till I tell you.'

There were footsteps on the stairs. Then the door was thrust open and Old Andrew came hurrying in.

'Papa,' cried Ernest.

The old man was in a dreadful state. His head was bare, and his white locks clung damply to his neck. He wore no coat or shoes, but was dressed in his house suit and thin slippers. His eyes were rolling wildly, and his mouth twitched uncontrollably. Andrew took no notice of his son but glanced past at Richard, who sat at his desk scrutinising him carefully. Martin had certainly got his craving, for Andrew Ledwhistle was indeed suffering. The old man lumbered forward and seized his arm in a weak grip.

'You, you swine,' he cried.

He started back, clutched his chest and swayed on his feet. Ernest sprang forward, and was just in time to catch him before he became unconscious.

Chapter 20

The doctor thrust his thumbs into the waistcoat pockets of his suit. He moved backwards and forwards, first on toes, then heels. The sun streamed through the window and glided over the face of the man on the bed. Old Andrew never moved. Only the bright look of burning intensity in his eyes betrayed that he lived, and was human. Oh, how that kindly face had altered in a night! The skin was a roll of parchment, yellow and frayed. The mouth, devoid of blood, hung open, and the hot tongue licked feverishly at the cracked lips. He never moved, and the blankets lay smooth as glass on his wasted body. The doctor's countenance was grave. He turned to Mary Ledwhistle, who knelt by the bed.

'Can you procure a lawyer right away?' he said. 'I do not think he will last the night.'

Chapter 21

It is night now, and the air is as rich and sparkling as the points of the many stars that twinkle in the velvet night. Round the bed kneel 7 people. Mrs Ledwhistle, her white cheeks sunken, clasps and unclasps the book in her hand. It is an old book, and was written when the world began. It has been shunned and sacrileged, loved and revered. It has been bound in silver and gold, cloth and paper, but the words inside hang clear and liquid like drops of blood of the one who died for us. Little Francis kneels beside his sisters, his little white face alone calm and serene. Death holds no terror for the very young, for they know not what it is. Ernest and Anna are together on their knees, while the figure on the bed speaks for the last time … in this world.

Old Andrew moves restlessly.

'Try hard, young Ernest,' he whispers. 'Try hard.'

He sinks back. There is a low moan from his wife.

'Andrew, Andrew.'

The name shivers in the air, and goes through the halls of memory, echoing hollowly. Let Richard Soleway hear that cry, and let him be haunted by it. 'Andrew, Andrew.' And Andrew Ledwhistle is dead.

Chapter 22

Rupert Bigarstaff rolled a wad of tobacco in his cheek, a habit he had gained from Gasper.

'It's no use,' he muttered. 'No use. It's true right enough.'

He watched the coffin lowered into the ground as the remains of Old Ledwhistle were put to rest. His eyes noted that Richard Soleway was not present.

It was a cold morning, yet early, and St Carthage's graveyard was in the open country. The sycamores waved softly, their maturing leaves tinged with a faint rusty gold. The scarlet poppies were waving in the tall grasses, and for once Bigarstaff felt at peace with other mortals. He thought that it would be nice to die in a place like this.

The tall-necked clergyman was plainly shivering. Silly devil, thought Bigarstaff, his blue eyes hard. He wanted to die when his body was tensed to the chill air, when the songs of the birds were clear and keen, when the blood was so red it hurt your flesh – not when the air was warm and sickly. He became aware that the last prayer had finished, and the mourners were alone. He'd wondered what they'd put on his headstone. One day he'd come back and see, but now, there was work to be done.

Meanwhile Richard was in his rooms. His head ached infernally, and his throat was dry. There was a knock at the door and a boy thrust his head round.

'Gent said as 'ow I was to give you this,' he said loudly.

'Name of Ledwhistle. He said you'd give me something no doubt.'

'Clear off,' cried Richard. 'Don't be a little liar.'

With a grin the boy went, and Richard was left alone. He slowly opened the long buff-coloured envelope, and drew out the contents. He started and nearly let the paper slip through his fingers, as the meaning soaked into the wool of his muddled brain.

You were left at your grandfather's death the sum of £45,000, but on the condition that you would enter the firm and make good. Owing to the bankruptcy of the firm that money can never be paid to you, or never will, owing to the fact that you ruined the name of Ledwhistle and Andromikey that my grandfather and yours made and founded. I can assure you that all this is true.

Ernest Ledwhistle.

For hours Richard sat slumped in his chair, his mind a blank. Finally, he drew a large sheet of paper towards him and began to write. When he had finished he folded it in four and put it in another envelope. Then he began his small amount of packing. In a cloth bag he pushed a couple of shirts and necessities and was ready.

He paid a call to a small bank, and then went to the shipping office. Here he booked a passage for America. He did not know that Gasper Liverwick and Rupert Bigarstaff did the same thing ... They were to cling to him for years to come.

Chapter 23

Robert Straffordson dragged himself wearily along the road, his wooden legs in monotonous rhythm clicking after him. His father, Radenstone, was in his house and Robert felt lost and tired. It was afternoon and warm. He wished he could do some work or try his hardest to be useful, but he was not strong enough yet to be this. In a fortnight's time he and his father were leaving for America, and this was what Straffordson was looking forward to.

He wondered as he walked along what Ernest Ledwhistle was going to do. He had met the boy many times and liked him. Mrs Ledwhistle was very poor now, and all the debts had not been paid. They were all too proud to accept aid or charity, and had been reduced to extenuating circumstances.

Straffordson wondered if he ought to go and see the family, when suddenly he caught sight of Fanny Ledwhistle and a young man he had come to know as James Coney. Fanny's hair hung in disordered array as usual, but the shapeless lips were parted a trifle and she gazed at James in a way that could not be mistaken.

Robert bowed as best he could, and the two smiled at him, while Coney bowed also.

'I hope your mother is in good health?' asked Robert.

Fanny sighed.

'Poor Mama is very dejected of late, for the house is to be sold, and we are to move into rooms. Mother is very much put about over good Jacob Steinhouse, for it was well known that Papa intended him to retire, and receive a considerable pension.' She sighed again as she continued. 'Martin Andromikey has not been seen of, and Jane says it is a good thing, for Ernest would surely set on him.'

James pressed his fingers in sympathy, which made that young lady conclude: 'Dear James has been so kind. Mama would have been quite lost without him, and as for me —'

She stopped, as if the very thought of such magnanimity was not to be dreamt of. Robert could not but repress a smile, for Fanny was so evidently adoring.

James said: 'Miss Ledwhistle was always a one for exaggeration.' This with a tender smile.

Fanny blushed and lowered her head modestly. Robert coughed, for laughter must surely be disguised.

'I hear,' said James pleasantly, 'that you are to leave for America soon, with your celebrated father.'

'Ah,' sighed he, 'America is a wonderful place. What part are you aiming to settle in?' (this was said with real interest).

Robert's reply was veiled. 'East,' he prevaricated. He did not want this boyish Coney to know where they were going. Radenstone and he wanted to leave behind all the old life and live together in Virginia.

He became aware that James was wishing him goodbye.

'We shall see you again before you go of course, Mr Straffordson,' simpered Fanny.

It was not long before they had disappeared out of sight and Robert was by himself again.

Chapter 24

Ernest waved his hand for the last time, and he and his sister moved away. On board the small sailing ship Radenstone turned to his son gladly.

'Last tie snapped, Rob,' he said quietly, 'and I for one feel better for it.'

In another part of the ship, leaning over the rough side, Richard Soleway watched England slip away on the horizon. He was not sorry. The land of his birth was nothing but a sordid incident, an incident which had cost an old man's life and his widow's happiness. He watched as the sullen green waters swirled gently against the sides, and heard behind him the shouts of the deck hands.

Down in the bowels of the same ship stood two men, Gasper and Rupert. They leant over the pens of some big brown cows and Rupert held his nose in the air pettishly.

'Devilishly airless hole,' he mumbled disdainfully.

Around them the livestock and cattle of the passengers were tethered. All were here, rending the air with their cries as the ship rolled under them. Gasper was silent. He could smell nothing, though the very air was foul. He slapped a big roan on its side, and laughed hoarsely as it quivered and flared its nostrils.

Bigarstaff retreated, and made for the passage. 'I'm going below,' he cried. 'Young Soleway isn't in the hold.'

Ah, miserable creatures of the hold! People who had not the

room of their thin beasts! Men and women whose faces were glowing with anticipation of the land that awaited them! They huddled together in the narrow hold, and tried to quench their hunger by dreaming of the fruit and fish they honestly thought would be theirs. They did not look up as Rupert entered, but went on staring with unseeing eyes, while their children slept uneasily in their mothers' laps.

Bigarstaff sat down and noted that nearly all were Irish. Now revolution had overtaken their country, and they were glad to leave. Up above in their secluded cabin Straffordson and his father were, and Bigarstaff envied them their space, but not their privacy. Alone, one is left to one's thoughts, while when a group of people surround you and take your interest things are forgotten and submerged.

Richard Soleway found no truth in that statement. As when alone, so was he tormented when he was in a crowd, for they seemed to glare with accusing eyes into his past. He shook his head in frenzy and tried to stamp all memories out.

Richard became aware that someone was at his elbow, and found the midnight visitor that had come so long ago at his side. He started, but was not afraid.

'Trying to forget Master Dicky, Richard?' said Gasper in a low voice.

'For God's sake stop persecuting me,' cried his victim. 'Leave me.'

Gasper smiled and never moved. His bantering grin was in Richard's vision and it danced before his eyes. His willpower snapped and his fist swept out. Then the two were rolling on the deck blow for blow, curse for curse, oath for oath. There was a cry from a deckhand and Captain Trevelian came hurrying. He was a cruel man, immensely tall and powerful. He swung Richard to his feet and gave him a brutal cut on the temple. Without a groan, Soleway hit the deck with a creaking of boards. Gasper was done the same to, and as he hit the deck

His will power
snapped.

he could hear the coarse yells of the crew, as oblivion swept over him.

When Gasper Liverwick awoke it was with a heavy pain in his head and an ache in his shoulders. He tried to move to relieve himself, but in vain. There were heavy manacles on his feet, and a length of rope round his arms. This rope looped through chains on his wrists and connected to his feet. He was on his back and his head bumped mercilessly on the timbers. By his side lay Richard also in irons, but he was unconscious and lying on his face. Liverwick could not but wince as the boy's features cracked with even constancy on the floor. They were in comparative darkness, which was not surprising, there being no portholes. Gasper shrewdly guessed it was night-time, and turned quickly as Richard gave a groan. The boy was in agony, for he had cramp, owing to the fact that the rope from shoulders to feet was drawn taut, curving his back. Gasper moved his body with difficulty and inserted his feet below Richard's stomach. He gave a heave, and Richard was also on his back. This seemed to ease him, but as yet he could not speak.

After a while he whispered. 'What is your name?'

'Gasper,' replied Liverwick cheerfully. 'How d'you feel, Mr Dicky?'

Richard when he spoke again sounded stronger. 'My head throbs like an old clock, and my back hurts deucedly bad,' he replied.

There was silence for a space. Then Liverwick said: 'How long d'you suppose they'll keep us ironed, me lad?'

'A couple of days, no more,' answered his fellow captive with confidence.

'Well, you're wrong,' cried Gasper. 'We're here for the trip. 'Tain't the first time I've been like this. Oh no, oh no. 'Tain't the first time.'

He could feel the boy's reaction and said in a gruff voice,

86

'Cheer up, Laddie. I tell you I've been in this way before, and I'm here to tell the tale.'

There was no reply, for Richard did not trust himself to speak. Finally, he sank into a painful slumber.

Gasper brought his head up with a shout. He had been awakened by the floor meeting his head with a thud, and he found himself rolling across the floor. In doing so he collided with Richard.

'Master Dick,' cried Liverwick loudly. 'Master Dick, what by all the saints is happening?'

He could hardly hear his own voice, for outside the wind was roaring and hissing, only equalled by the noise of the sea.

Richard came in contact with a bar of wood and clenched his hands. They were both in an intolerable position, for they were at the sea's mercy. Up above they could hear dimly the noises of the animals, and the shouts that came from the hold above them. Then Gasper gave a panic-stricken shriek as there was the sound of a pistol above.

'My God, Richard,' he yelled. 'They're shooting the beasts. We're sinking, we're sinking.'

His voice was partly lost, but the significance was there, and Richard Soleway paled. There was a sudden crack, a break. Then the ship lurched as the mainstay mast came crashing down. There were shouts on deck as every man struggled for a seat in the boats.

'Let us out,' screeched Gasper, 'you dirty cowards. Let us out, for God's sake. Let us out.'

His voice faded away and he choked.

There was a swelling sob from Richard. 'They can't leave us like rats,' he breathed. 'They can't. Help, Help.' But his voice was only a pathetic whisper.

'Rupert, Rupert,' cried Gasper tearingly. 'Oh my God, let me out, let me out.' His last words hung in the air and shivered away. 'Oh God,' he groaned. 'Oh, oh aaa, ohm.'

Backwards and forwards they rolled, and they both tried franticaly to release their bonds. There was a pain-laden scream from Richard as his back was nearly bent double by his struggles. His head came with a muffled thud on a metal case, and for the second time he was unconscious. When he stirred the boat was swaying gently.

'Gasper,' he said faintly.

Then came the reply: 'You're lucky, man. You slept through the storm. We are on some rocks, and if we don't get out of this soon it's be all up with us.'

Richard could hardly believe his ears. He began to struggle hard, but was bade be still by his 'friend'.

'Don't hurt yourself,' cried Liverwick. 'I'm lying on my face by a nail, and with luck it will fray this rope.'

'It will take hours,' said Richard in despair once more. 'The rope is thick and hard.'

'So's my faith,' came the answer, and Richard was silent.

And so, four hours later, Gaspar broke the rope that kept his hands to his feet. He put his arms above his head and slowly got to his feet, only to collapse.

'Steady,' warned Richard. This time Gasper wormed his way along the floor and gripped the boy's bonds. It was a difficult job to untie the knots, for his hands were handcuffed together, but at last it was done, and they were both partly free.

'We can't walk,' cried Richard, 'for our feet are in chains, but we can hop.'

They felt in the dingy light for the door and put their shoulders to the wood. Many times they collapsed and lay prone, but they always tried again, and at last the lock burst and they stumbled over the threshold. The light streamed down to them and they were half blinded. Up the steps they painfully went, and saw the animals lying stiff and cold in their stalls.

At last they reached the deck, and Richard gave a great shout.

'Land,' he gasped. 'We're on a beach. We're saved. Land.'

He fell on his knees and Gasper gazed awkwardly at him.

'Oh dear God,' cried Richard joyfully. 'We thank Thee for deliverance. Amen.'

'Amen,' said Gasper gruffly and wiped his eyes.

Chapter 25

The beach was white and fine, and, as it stretched beneath some green and sparkling trees, turned a soft yellow. The sun shone on wild flowers and dense woods, while the water around, lapping on the shingle, was a clear and radiant green.

Gasper bit his lip at the scene.

Richard too was overcome, but finally he turned and said: 'Gasper, my friend, we must find some tools that will free us from these encumbrances.'

They hopped along, and by mid-day – or so they guessed it to be – they were unshackled and free. They ran shouting to the side of the wrecked boat and raced madly up the shingle. Richard threw himself down and drank and drank the cool water that was in abundance.

When they had drunk their fill they looked about them and measured up their surroundings. Before was a great mass of trees, and to the right were two big islands.

'Well, seeing as 'ow we're here,' said Gasper heartily, 'we might as well eat. Let's get back to the boat, for there's plenty of good meat.'

'Look,' cried Richard. 'First I will build a fire, while you bring a calf or pig.'

So Gasper made for the boat while Richard busied himself collecting wood.

Richard found his flint had gone, but on striking his ring

A queer friendship sprang
up between the two men.

against the heel of his shoe a flame was soon burning, and then a fire.

Gasper came back across the sand bearing on his shoulders a calf and holding under his arm a knife. Richard would have draped the calf over the fire, but Gasper stayed him, laughed his great rumbling laugh.

'First we must skin him,' he cried, and set about it.

When it had been cleaned, he laid it down and looked about him. On arriving on the island they had been amazed by the giant shells covering the ground. The smallest was the size of a tray. Gasper seized one in his arms and put two stones on either side of the fire. In these he placed the shell, the outside crust to the heat. In this way the calf was hung on a platter above the flames.

'If you put the meat on top of the fire,' shouted Gasper, 'you'll char it and put the fire out as well. Now those stones keep the shell from resting on the wood, and so the meat will be browned in no time.'

Richard did not know what to say. 'To be sure, Gasper, you're a treasure, and no mistake.'

The roasted beef was succulent and juicy, and both tucked in with a will. Then the fire was put out and they rolled into the shade of the trees to sleep. They slept till evening, and they found the air was chill.

'We must get some shot and ball from the ship,' advised Richard. 'There may be inhabitants, or wild animals. It's best to be prepared.'

Back to the boat they trudged and got some pistols.

'There is enough wood to make a small boat,' said Gasper.

'They collected blankets and more food and found to their amazement that a cow was lustily bellowing. They hurriedly untethered her and watched her go lumberingly up the beach. Then they gathered knives, a cask of butter, salt and a barrel of ale – this Richard was loath to take, knowing what mischief it could do, but Gasper was equally loath to leave it behind – and a saw. A saw, as Gasper pointed out, was very important.

With these they staggered up the sand and set them down. A cool wind was blowing from the sea, and neither felt disposed to sleep. So they each armed themselves with a gun and set off. Judging by the height and colour of the sun, Gasper guessed the time to be about 9, and there hung over the island that refreshing keenness that belongs to night.

They plunged through the wood and gazed about them, at the beauteous flowers and vines. Little streams gushed by them, and brightly feathered birds flew chatteringly by. They were very wild and scared, and that made the two doubly sure the island was uninhabited. At the other side of the wood came the sea again and, branching to their right, they could see nestling in the translucent waters the other two islands. They came to the shore and, being tired, sat for a long while on a square piece of land that later became known as the Rum Cove. It grew dark but still they sat on, and a queer friendship sprang up between the two men.

Suddenly Richard gave a shout. 'Look,' he yelled, 'the sea's parting and there's a strip of land from this isle to the next.'

Richard was all for journeying across that night, but Gasper was older and wiser and would not hear of it.

That night they slept by the east shore, and for once Richard forgot his misery and was happy.

Chapter 26

When he awoke, the sun was very high, and he heard the clear notes of a bird by his head. Looking up, he saw a bright blue head, and a green body. Sticking up from his head was a brilliant tuft of feathers. His little yellow eyes glittered, and his throat visibly swelled as the lonely notes rang out.

Richard propped himself on one elbow and gave a sigh of contentment. Gasper was nowhere in sight as he scrabbled hastily to his feet. Through the trees came he soon and he carried a large shell. As he hailed Richard, the boy saw it was full of milk, and guessed the cow had supplied it.

'Dick,' cried Gasper, 'will you go and gather some fruit. There's plenty if you look.'

Richard did look and came back laden with some green kind of apples and also some very small potatoes or taros. These were cooked as before, and when they tried the apples they proved very sweet and nourishing.

After this repast they hurried to the NE of the island to Rum Cove. But they could not find that strip of sand and Gasper Liverwick reasoned that the tides were irregular.

'It will probably be uncovered tonight,' he supplied.

'When can we get out of here?' asked Richard as they sat down. 'We can't stay here for the rest of our lives.'

'I wonder what happened to the captain and the crew?' said the other. 'That crew, that captain – if this were England they'd be put in jail for what they did. We could build a boat,

Dick, but we have no compass and do not know where we are. We can only hope a ship will pass by.'

'What do you think our chances are?' was Richard's next question.

Gasper did not reply at once. Instead he gazed far out at sea, and his whiskers fluffed dreamily.

'I don't know,' he said at length. 'I don't know.'

Then he got to his feet and stretched himself. 'Stir yourself Dick. We must see what shape the old ship's in. We could make her seaworthy in a couple of months, if there be nothing really amiss.'

The boat lay on her side, in the fine sand, her deck strewn with wreckage, her bottom partly stove in. The two went below into the cabin of Radenstone and his son and searched around for some clue as to who had occupied it. In one of the drawers by the ruined bunk a pistol was brought to light, a bible such as mariners carry, and a dog-eared book. Richard opened this at once, while beneath him, Gasper Liverwick busied himself with the dead animals.

As he turned the pages a scrap of paper fluttered out, and quickly he bent to pick it up. It was a picture, and Richard felt a queer intake of breath go through his chest as he saw the figure of a man on a cross. Below, there were some words in French. He deciphered with difficulty: 'Father, forgive them, for they know not what they do.' He put it down swiftly and turned away. He swallowed, turned back and put the paper inside the Bible.

Then he sat down and opened the other book once more. The second page was blank except for a small square in the top right-hand corner and Richard frowned as he read: 'Solomon Pertwee, Yyankskee Villa, Lower Yangtsee, China.' He turned over rapidly and found that the middle pages contained cuttings. The writing was not English, but plainly Chinese characters. Richard's brow wrinkled as he saw written in the margin in faded writing; 'Map on back of Crucifiction.' He grew interested and fumbled eagerly for the picture he had pushed into the Bible. Turning it over he saw the map.

'Gasper,' he shouted, 'Gasper, quick, quick!'

He brought his foot down on the wood and his very skin seemed to tremble with excitement.

Gasper burst through the door.

Before he could speak, Richard had thrust the map before his eyes. 'Don't you see?' he cried. 'It's the island, this island! There's the cove where the strip of land appeared, and there's the other islands to the North East.'

His friend peered at it unbelievingly.

'Where did you get it?' he asked incredulously.

'In this cabin,' Richard cried. 'Gasper, what could it mean?'

'See if there's a name in that Bible,' Gasper advised. But before his friend could do this, he had picked it up.

'Quick,' he cried. 'What does it say?'

'*Victor Radenstone 1826*. Why,' cried Richard, 'I've met this man. He was in China through the Opium War. What is the connection though between him and Solomon Pertwee?' He chaffed irritably. 'If only I could understand Chinese.'

'Isn't there any English in that diary?' cried Gasper in a great state.

'There is not,' was the answer. 'But look, there are some arrows between the second and third island.'

'There should be arrows from this island to the next,' cried Gasper, 'but not from the second to the third. Unless of course there's another sea-causeway. We'll soon know anyhow, for we'll cross that strip tonight if it appears.'

They waited in a fever of impatience till sundown and then made their way to the East side of the island. But the sea stretched away to the other two islands in an unbroken carpet.

At Gasper's suggestion they waited till the moon arose, and

finally, when the first star had climbed to its appointed place, the stretch was parted and the firm ground once more was there. In silence the two men walked over, and placed their feet on the second island. This was the same as its brother, but very much smaller. As they neared the middle, the trees grew thicker and then ended suddenly. The moon shone on a piece of grass-waste and they did not halt but strode on. There was a sudden scream from Richard, and Gasper was in time to see him sinking into the ground.

'Marsh,' he groaned, then raced to one side.

With much difficulty a very shaken Richard was hauled out of the treacherous mud.

'It didn't look dangerous,' protested Richard as, coated with green slime, he followed Gasper.

They skirted the marsh and came to the end once more. But no strip of land confronted them, so they moved along to the North. After walking for a short space they came to a steep hill. On climbing it, they beheld the sea, and here they saw another causeway.

'W-ell.' Hesitatingly Gasper Liverwick looked across to the third island. The moon had gone behind a bank of clouds, and the island looked grey and sharp.

'Come on,' cried Richard. 'Let's cross at once.'

Gasper Liverwick followed reluctantly.

Chapter 27

Robert Straffordson lay in the bottom of the small boat, his useless legs flat out before him. Beside him sat his father, while, his hawk-like face set in a black scowl, Captain Trevelian crouched in the stern. Five members of the rough crew were rowing strongly, and over to their right the second boat could be seen. Robert wore a white-set expression, and his father was the same. Now and again the two cast contemptuous glances at the rascally captain. Trevelian was aware of these looks and inwardly he cursed savagely. Doubtless those men he had locked in the hold had drowned, but father and son were safe, weren't they? Blast them. What did they think he was, a cushy owner of a luxury ship? He was responsible for his boat, and dammit but he'd get it when they reached land again – if we ever do, he thought, grimly gazing at the bleak outline of the unknown coast they were drawing nigh to. He shivered a little as he thought of the two poor devils locked behind in the hold. He huffed his shoulders. It wasn't the first time men had disappeared at sea. He wasn't caring, or was he?

They passed a finger of rocky land, and drew into a small bay. Stiffly Trevelian climbed onto the shingle and issued his orders. Two more boatfuls of men rowed in, and they moved off in a solid body inland. Rupert Bigarstaff found himself marching by Radenstone and son. He looked upward at the heavens and thought 'Old Gasper's getting his due, Lord.' He chuckled, as Robert limped along beside him, his wooden peg stumps sinking into the white sand.

Trevelian called a halt shortly, and they made camp for the night. Once one of the deck hands tenderly enquired about food, but no one seemed disposed to wander about this grim, rocky little island. So, rolled on the sparse ground, they slept till morning.

When light invaded their slumber, Robert woke to see a barren rocky land about him. Unlike its brothers, this island was not covered in tall trees and vegetation. He saw Trevelian standing with a knot of his crew, talking and deliberating. Rupert Bigarstaff was not with them, but was sitting on a boulder staring with a fiendish grin on his face at the group.

His father was nowhere in sight and he struggled to get to his feet. Bigarstaff strolled over to him and stretched forth his hands, and with hesitation Robert took them. When he was half on his feet, Rupert let go suddenly and Robert fell sharply, to lie helplessly on his back. With a laugh Bigarstaff walked back to his old seat and seemed to forget everything immediately.

Foolishly, Robert scrambled gamely to his feet and walked away. He cursed himself for his disability, as he shambled on, and not for the first time fell to thinking on Jane Ledwhistle. Then he saw his father and he was carrying a flask of clear water and a bunch of carrots.

'Good heavens,' cried Robert. 'Where on earth did you get those vegetables, Father?'

Radenstone smiled. 'Over in a sandy patch in the North side,' he provided. 'You know, Rob, I can't help thinking that someone was wrecked on this island like we are. Otherwise how are these –' pointing to the large carrots, '– to be explained?'

'Well,' answered Robert, his eyes lighting, 'whoever planted them is not here now. That means there's hope for us.'

They had by this time reached a small cave and, sitting down, began their meal. Flat yet sharp land sloped before them to the sea, and Victor remarked thoughtfully, 'You know, Rob, I have a feeling that I know this island, or at least by sight.'

His son gaped stupidly. 'What?'

'In China, some years ago,' said Radenstone, 'I met a man named Pertwee, Solomon Pertwee.'

Robert listened with interest.

'You see,' continued his father, 'being a missionary I met all sorts of people, and it was at a local function of other men in the same calling as myself that I met this man. He was small, very bald, and he wore no wig of any sort. I became very friendly with him, and he with me. During our friendship he told me of his life, and when he died he left me a small map of a group of islands. He said that on the third island to the extreme north he made a valuable oil discovery. His greatest ambition, he said, was to return to the island and stake his claim, thereby giving him the money which would bring relief to the people he devoted himself to. He said he wished me one day to journey there in his place. Ah, he was a good man —' this with a wistful note creeping into his voice.

'But Father,' interposed Robert excitedly, 'if this is the island, where is the oil? Have you the map?'

'Steady on, my boy.' But Radenstone himself found he was being carried away. 'Unfortunately it was in my cabin when we took to the boats,' he cried, and his voice sank to a mere whisper. 'It's gone below with those other two poor devils.'

Before they could say more there was a sound of lusty bellowing, and turning they faced Trevelian and his crew. Of Bigarstaff there was no sign.

The captain strode up with a bloated and annoyed countenance, and cried angrily enough. 'Look here, Mr Radenstone, Sir, you can't be going and slipping away like

100

this. Mebbe you're a gentleman of quality and all, but on an island, God knows where, we're all alike, and must act as such. Now see this, Mr Radenstone, I'm the captain, and you takes orders from me along with the rest o' them.'

He rounded this off with such a superior and brutal air that Radenstone flushed and could barely suppress striking the man.

Robert looked shrewdly at the bully seaman. He wondered just how much had been overheard. He looked past at the crew, and at one man in particular. He was an ordinary deckhand, an old man with clouded eyes, and crinkled lips. His round arms were bare to the elbow, a ruddy brown and freckled all over. The rough shirt displayed a broad expanse of chest, deep and muscular and covered in fine hair. There was a look of disdain on his face as he looked at his captain. With a final sneer on his countenance Trevelian turned. His crew followed him, but the sailor made no effort to move.

'Mr Radenstone, sir,' he said hoarsely, and he spoke with a rich Scottish accent.

Robert waited expectantly and he was not disappointed.

'I'm very much afraid that Trevelian plans to do you harm, sir,' said the deckhand.

Radenstone paled.

'I feared as much,' he answered. 'What is your name?'

'John Pearson Sir.'

'Well, Mr Pearson, would you be so good as to tell me and my son what you know, for I do not think you also wish us ill.'

'Indeed I do not,' protested John Pearson, his honest face worried. 'You see, we were all listening when you were telling young Mr Radenstone about the map and the oil. Captain Trevelian plans to get your map and find the oil for himself and he's promised the lads a share if we help him.'

'But I haven't —'

Before he could continue, Robert cut into his father's

101

sentence. 'He won't get it in a hurry, I can assure you, John Pearson. Father will keep a good hold on it. But how do they plan to get it?'

Pearson shrugged his shoulders and under his tan he whitened. 'I wouldna like to say, but he'll stick at nothing.'

There was a sudden roar from the other direction.

'Captain wants me, no doubt,' he said.

Father and son watched him walk briskly away.

'Why did you not want him to know about the map?' asked Radenstone, when the burly form was lost from sight.

'Listen, Papa,' Robert said. 'If they think we have the map they won't start pumping for the oil just yet. We can stave them off for the time being with words, and also begin looking for the stuff ourselves. Look, Father, you've got to use your memory. What spot was the oil marked at?'

'But Robert,' gasped Radenstone. 'Don't you see what will happen to us? Even if we did strike the oil, how could we get off the island? We've no ship, we don't know even where we are, and we're hopelessly outnumbered.'

'Think, Papa, think,' urged Robert. 'Where did the oil mark come on the island? You've got to think. We must find the oil before them. They'll want to get off the island as much as we, so they'll make provisions. Now think. Think.'

Chapter 28

Radenstone looked anxiously at Robert Straffordson.

'Robert,' he said in a whisper, 'I don't like the look of it at all. I don't like it at all.'

Captain Trevelian and his roughened crew were seated on one side of a roaring fire. The faces glowed blackly and the shadows flickered and leapt on their countenances. They muttered and talked to each other. Rupert Bigarstaff looked on, a queer smile on his fiendish face, and Straffordson and Radenstone felt very uneasy. They had been on the island two days and a night and the men had grown increasingly restless as the hours had passed.

Suddenly there was a fierce shout from a look-out, and a sound of shouts. Trevelian sprang to his feet and looked wildly round, brandishing his sword. Through the darkness and into the firelight blundered two men in the grip of three stalwart deckhands.

'Gasper, my lad,' said Rupert softly, without the slightest surprise in his voice.

'Martin Andromikey,' gasped Radenstone.

'God in Heaven,' swore Trevelian with an oath. 'You?'

Gasper looked round and his eyes fell on Rupert Bigarstaff. Something pulled at his mouth, and it twitched uncontrollably. His head seemed to jerk back on his spine, and he shuddered as he caught the smouldering carnal green light in those eyes.

103

Richard Soleway switched himself forward and stuck his head out. 'You devil,' he hissed, 'you devil.'

Trevelian fell back a pace. He flourished his sword and began his blustering. The three stalwarts gripped Richard's arms and twisted them behind his back brutally.

Richard did not wince, though his eyes grew pinched. 'You devilish swine,' he said between clenched teeth.

This time he had cause to scream, and fell prostrate.

Straffordson stumbled forward. 'Leave him alone,' he shouted.

At that moment of tenseness anything could have happened. Then Rupert Bigarstaff the orator stepped forward and nothing did.

'Now, now,' he said, his voice a sea of velvet, 'don't let's be hasty.'

On and on he droned, and soon everyone was sullenly quiet. For the life of them they could not think how this small man had the power to rule over their wills.

When he had finished, Rupert Bigarstaff strolled away, and watched the great black clouds swirl above him. Radenstone pressed Richard's arm eagerly, and tried to forget that this one boy had been the cause of Old Andrew Ledwhistle's death.

'How on earth,' he cried, 'did you cross to here?'

Gasper pulled a bedraggled paper from his pocket. ''Ere's how we got across,' he said. 'We found this map in your cabin, Sir.' Robert staggered inwardly. Too late. There was a savage cry from Trevelian and the crew as they fell onto them, with guttural oaths.

Desperately they fought, but to no avail. Ropes were knotted round them, and they lay helpless on the ground, while Captain Trevelian grasped the chart with trembling fingers.

'Ah,' he cried, 'at last. We must begin work at once. We will cross to the other islands, and see if there are any materials for making picks and swords.'

Trevelian led his men over the causeways, and finally landed on the first isle.

Here in due course the old ship was sighted.

'We must repair her at once,' cried Trevelian. 'Now make yourselves useful.'

So in the light of the moon they began their task.

By dawn the animals were all out of the ship, and rope, pistols and the like had been carefully sorted. The Captain straightened his back thankfully.

'We can go back now,' he said. 'Those four will be getting restless.'

Talking and laughing, he led the men over the land. But the sea was not obligingly parted as before.

'By Heaven,' thundered Trevelian, 'we're trapped.' He grew steadier. 'It must be the tides,' he said wildly. 'You, Carson, stand post, and call us if the strip appears.'

Moodily they were marched back, and the unrelenting Captain kept them hard at it all day. A young bullock was roasted and torn asunder in greedy haste.

'By heck,' ejaculated Trevelian, 'but these dead animals are useful. But we must salt them, for already the flesh is rotting.'

'It's no wonder, is it, lads,' cried one Timothy Birney, the thin first mate, 'that those two dogs didn't go hungry.'

'Look here, Captain,' said another. 'How are we to know the oil be there?'

'We won't, till we've dug up every bit of the island,' answered Trevelian curtly. 'And look here, me lads. If you'll stick by me, I'll stand by you.'

'Aye, we will, Cappen, we will,' assented his crew.

Aye, poor devils they can hardly refuse.

'When do you think the boat'll be fit for the sea, me lads?' asked Trevelian shortly.

He turned round and looked at the tossed black-timbered bulk.

'I shouldn't be surprised if we could have it ready in little over a week,' said the second mate. 'There's lots of new boards needed, and a mast, as well as a sail. Reckon her stern be stove in, but there's plenty of timber about, so it can't be such a job.'

'What about the money from the oil, Cappen?'

'What about that, eh?' put in another, his eyes glittering. 'You're sure you'll go halves with us?'

'Sure. You heard me give me word before,' thundered Trevelian. 'Now be content, and stir yourselves there. Come on. There's work to be done.'

Chapter 29

It is a fortnight later. In a rudely constructed hut lie four men – our four unfortunates.

The air was very close and hot, and not a breath of wind stirred. Overhead black clouds were gathering, and all was still and hushed, as if waiting for something.

'If only they'd make their move,' cried Richard at last, his brow furrowed with the heat.

The others made no reply but sat moodily brooding over their captivity. There was rustling outside and Johnny Pearson crept in. The others started hopefully.

'Now listen carefully,' cried the deckhand. 'The oil has been struck down to the south of the island. The boat's finished, and they intend to leave tonight.'

'But what about us?' gasped Radenstone weakly.

'You are to be disposed of,' was the grim answer. 'But listen. When it is dark I will come and let you loose. No more canna do. You must board the ship if you can without their knowledge.'

'But where is the boat,' hissed Gasper. 'Tell us that, John Pearson.'

'It's moored in a bay on the southern coast on the first island. They reckon it'll be safer to start from there, for the rocks round here are pretty treacherous. But there's one thing – once I cut you free, you're on your own. It's more than I can risk to aid you farther.'

'Thank you, thank you,' cried Radenstone. 'I promise that if we get to England safely, you'll benefit by it.'

'I dinna want no riches,' was the rough answer. 'All I want is my neck. Ye understand.' He cast a scared glance behind him, and the next moment had gone.

'Do you think we'll manage it,' asked Robert eagerly. 'How can we get food?'

Thus they talked in excited whispers, and mostly about their chances and about the oil. Darkness increased and the four could hear the shouts of the captain and his crew on the shore. Through the gloom crept Pearson. In his hand he clasped a large knife, and it was the work of a moment for the ropes to be sliced.

As he cut, he whispered, 'I was sent to kill you. If Trevelian finds you on board, your throats and mine will surely be slit. For God's sake, be careful.'

Then, hurrying away, he left them to themselves.

'Follow me,' cried Richard, as he led the way. The white moon sailed supreme, and caught a bright metallic glitter in the water. The sea lay dangerously passive and gave hardly a ripple as they crept over the rocky ground.

They came to the causeway and padded over. Suddenly, a sound of curses broke the stillness, and looking back they glimpsed black silhouettes leaping over the beach. With dismay they began to run, but Robert Straffordson was a great handicap. Before they reached the other side of the sandy strip the figures were some 200 yards behind them. Panting, Gasper reached the side strip and helped the stumbling Robert. Over the causeway came the crew, led by Trevelian. Richard, grunting, his breath coming in great tearing gasps, raced along. The sharp thuds that came from his feet landing on the hard grass of the second island went in rhythm with the beats of his heart, which seemed to be swimming in a sea of red heat. There were more shouts, that rang out very clear in the

Into the lucious
green they went.

tropical night, and their pursuers were very close.

'The bog,' screamed Gasper. 'Let them outrun you.'

For a split-second Richard just let his legs carry him. Then he realised what was meant by that statement. Catching the hobbling Robert and his father by the shoulders, he jerked to a stop. Past them went Trevelian and his men. Into that luscious green they went. Trevelian's guttural bass rose to a gurgling treble as he sank to his knees. Struggling, he began to scream. By his side fought John Pearson. With a savage shriek Trevelian brought his knife up and stabbed it into the breast of the deckhand. Richard felt his stomach lurch as the moon shone on the rich red blood that flowed like wine from the gash. With one last agonised curse, the rascally captain sank from sight. Richard had the impression of a quiet bubbling stretch of mud. Then he was running again. Behind four men strode, the only remnants of the crew to escape such a terrifying end. Through the trees the chase went on. Down a hill and over the second causeway. Far behind came the oaths of their pursuers.

'Look,' gasped Radenstone. 'The gap's closing. The tide's moving over it. Hurry, run.'

It was true. With desperate speed, their legs moving like pistons, they flew along. A 100 yards or so from the causeway came the last four of the crew. Then they were over, and the sea lay in a sheet over the lane of sand.

'We're safe,' screamed Robert.

'We've got to keep on running,' panted Gasper. 'Those sailors can swim. Look, the boat.'

Moored to a rocky cleft lay the ship.

'There's a wind coming,' cried Radenstone. 'Oh thank God, thank God.'

With fumbling fingers Gasper Liverwick untied the rope, while Richard and Radenstone, helped by Robert, hauled up the sail. A queer sail it was too – a sheet of animal hide – but as the first puff of wind caught it she billowed and the ship was putting out.

At the wheel Gasper sank his head on his arms. 'Oh Jesus,' he moaned. 'Thanks be.' He thought of the eyes of Rupert Bigarstaff and gave thanks again.

The dangerous calm of the hour before had justified its warning. Irritable flicks of wave stung the ship's sides, and a few spots of rain began to fall. From the shore came great shouts.

'Never mind them,' yelled Robert. 'There's plenty of food for them, so they shan't starve.'

'What a night, Andromikey,' gasped Radenstone. 'Poor Pearson, poor Pearson.'

'There's a storm arising,' shouted Gasper. 'Slacken the main sail.'

This was duly done, and it was just in time, for a great gust of wind struck the ship and sent her prancing through the waves. Drenched to the skin, their hearts alight with hope, they waited for the morn.

Chapter 30

For three days and nights the storm raged, but on the fourth morning they awoke from their stupor to calm skies and unruffled waters. Robert Straffordson rubbed his eyes hard, and moved his wooden pegs. On the horizon he glimpsed a fine sailing ship, and he let out a hoarse cry.

'A ship,' he cried. 'Father, Gasper, look, look – a ship!'

Stumbling up, he raced to Liverwick, who lay against the boat's side, straining his eyes.

'You're right, lad,' he said huskily. 'A French craft, by the look of things.'

By now Richard Soleway and Radenstone had joined them.

'Raise a flag or sign,' cried the frenzied Robert. 'They must see us.'

'They will. Never fear,' cried Radenstone. 'They'll draw near in an hour or two's time, see if they don't.'

Shortly after 10, or so they judged it to be, they were within earshot of the French ship. A thin boy in a ragged shirt stood by the bows.

'English,' he called, cupping his hands together.

The sound had no time to fade, before Gasper yelled, 'Yes, can you take us on board? Our craft's in bad trim.'

The boy turned to the cluster of sailors on board, and a peak-capped man who was evidently the captain.

There was a consultation which took so long that Richard yelled out, 'Where are we?'

'About 180 miles from Cape Verdi Islands,' answered the boy.

The captain raised his voice. 'Come across,' he said with difficulty. 'My ship will come by yours. Draw in.'

They did, and the slight handsome captain boarded their boat. They made a queer group of men. Robert, a rent in his trouser leg showing a stretch of wood; Gasper, his rascally face partly hid by a three-weeks growth of beard; Radenstone, his big brown hands twitching; and Richard, wearing a sullen dogged expression, because for the first time in a fortnight the memory of Andrew Ledwhistle had again risen in his mind.

'Tous Anglais?' asked the Frenchman, and they nodded, or Richard did.

'War has been declared between the Russians and our people and yours,' said the captain.

Radenstone clasped the hand-rail. The rest said nothing. The Crimean War had begun. Their men would fight the stocky, solid, dissipated Russians: the cold, stout foreigners against the awkward bull-complexioned Britishers.

The handsome captain looked at them curiously and shrugged his shoulders affectedly.

''Tis très sad,' he murmured. He swept a pair of coal-black eyes over them. 'You are in need of food,' he said softly. 'Yes?'

They nodded dumbly.

'One of my men shall stay here in charge.' He lapsed into French and called something out.

Stiffly the four climbed to the other boat and watched three slim sailors man their own. They were led below and food was set before them. The white-faced boy sat with them. They learnt that his name was Jim Racliff.

'I went to sea when I was 15,' he told them. 'Captain is a good man and kind.'

They in their turn told them their story, and summoned the

French captain. The map was brought out and the captain grew greatly excited.

'A find indeed,' he stuttered. 'Good sirs, permit.' He turned to Jim and spoke hurriedly. 'The captain begs that he should take you back to England and set out with an expedition to stake the oil,' interpreted Jim slowly.

Chapter 31

It is the year 1857 in the month of January.

There was in the room of a certain building down Pentworth Street a great bustling and removing. Hammers hammered, screws screwed, nails nailed and the like, as well as a hundred other such things. Richard Soleway stood by the door, sleeves rolled up and his hair on end. With him stood Gasper Liverwick. If Old Andrew had been alive, his diary would have been well-stocked. Three years ago the Crimean War had begun. The papers had been full of Palmerston, a plain woman called Nightingale or some such name, Sidney Herbert and many more. Two years ago Victor Radenstone and Robert Straffordson had gone to live on the New Era Isle. Less than a year ago the French Captain Defause and Liverwick and Soleway had located the oil, and claims had been staked. Radenstone had divided the oil between Defause, Gasper and Soleway. He had himself given a sum of money to the Chinese Missionary Society, and Richard was now a very rich man.

Gasper turned to his friend. 'What name shall we put on the door, Dick?'

'No name whatever as yet,' answered Richard. 'In another ten years or so I may put something up.' He took his coat off his peg and struggled into it. 'Yes,' he said softly. 'Maybe I will in ten years or so.'

Chapter 32

Phillip Hobart turned round to his friend Henry Cordane and said reflectively: 'That unnamed firm in Pentworth Street is doing damned well. They handled Crewell Newbolt's case last week.'

Cordane shrugged his slim shoulders. 'Really?' he yawned. 'I say, old chappie, your date's wrong. It's June 11th 1862 not July 7th.'

* * *

The firm of Gladridges and Wilkinson held a board meeting in the year 1879. 'We are met,' said the Chairman, 'to decide what we are to do in this great crisis. What can we do to keep our name? The Pentworth lawyers must be equalled.'

Chapter 33

Richard Soleway pushed a greying lock of hair back from off his forehead. He looked his 55 years, and the old man by his side shook his head.

'You need a holiday, Dick.'

Old Gasper Liverwick sounded concerned. He was 72, with a head of black hair not lightened by even a rumour of whiteness. The hands of the one-time sea-dog were traced with heavy purple veins, but they did not shake.

Richard leaned back in his chair and looked around him. 'Yes,' he said. 'And I'm going to have it. In a month's time we can leave this place and settle down far away.'

'You mean the business is all ready for Ernest Ledwhistle and his son?' asked Gasper heavily. He knew he did not need an answer. The last 30 years had been spent in hard brain-work with hardly a break. It had all been done for Ernest Ledwhistle and his son James, and now the task had been accomplished and they could rest.

Ernest sat in an office too that afternoon, but he was sick at heart. He had for 11 years sat at this high desk totting up figures. His mother was still alive, a frail voluptuous senile old hag of nearly 80. The years and the poverty had not gone well with her. She would at this moment be with Anna in their pokey little parlour, for she lived with them now. His son James would not be at home. He would be at least growing strong and healthy in Virginia along with Charles Coney, his sister's boy. His memory drifted back to the days when Francis had been but seven and James barely two. James Coney had come in and Old Andrew had thanked him profusely. He remembered with a sudden smile how Fanny had blushed and how Charlotte had stuffed her sampler into her mouth. '30 years ago,' he sighed. '30 years ago –' his face darkened – 30 years ago Martin Andromikey had killed his father. He had brought shame and suffering to his poor old mother, and caused her mentality. But for Martin Andromikey, Francis would not be an incurable drunkard. But for Martin Andromikey –

His hands fell forward onto the desk and he groaned hopelessly. 30 years ago all his castles had been brought crashing to the ground, by that same Martin Andromikey. 'And 30 years from now,' he whispered, 'please God I shall be dead.' And Jane and Francis, Charlotte and James, what were they going to be? 'Oh God,' he muttered. 'Oh God.'

Chapter 34

London
    October 18th
Dear James,
This letter will be a great surprise to you no doubt but a
pleasant surprise. 3 weeks ago I was handed the Pentworth
firm. The mysterious owners disappeared leaving a
document that entitled me to the business. Come home at
once, son, for I wish to set up. Charles is needed too. Your
mother has written to your aunt. Will expect you as soon as
possible.

Yours affectionately, Father.

This extraordinary letter James Ledwhistle read out to his
cousin Charles.

'What on earth do you make of that?' gasped he in
amazement. 'It's incoherent. Come home at once.'

Charles broke out in a delighted laugh. 'Think of it, Jim,' he
cried. 'Just think of it. I can leave Father's shop and join forces
with you, as Uncle suggests. Come, I want to talk to Mama.'

He led the way out of the room and they found Fanny
seated on a couch sorting out some bills. But can this be the
perspiring Fanny Ledwhistle of old? Where is the flustered
stoutness, the foolish gaze? Certainly not in this competent
matronly woman with the grey hair.

Her son waved the letter in front of her and sat down beside her.

'Mother,' he cried. 'Mother, is it true? Am I to go to England with James? Tell me, am I?'

The busy figure said primly, 'Yes, Charles, you are. I should hardly have expected you to show joy at leaving your home.'

Before her son could reply, James Coney came into the room.

'So you know about it at last do you lads?' he said.

James had not altered. The grey hair hung jaggedly over his eyes and his long wrists shunned his coat sleeves.

'Uncle James,' asked young Ledwhistle perplexedly. 'What does it all mean? Has Father been left this – this Pentworth firm? And if he has, why? What does anyone know about Papa, that they should let him inherit this business? He's only a clerk.'

'It's quite true though, boy,' replied Coney. 'From what I can gather from your father's somewhat incoherent and muddled letter, these lawyers have totally disappeared leaving only this deed proclaiming a transfer of ownership.'

He turned to Charles and said somewhat drily: 'It's your chance to get out of the shop and incidentally your social rut.'

Fanny's lips tightened. If she had been a coquette, with perhaps some reason for being one, she would have tossed her head. James Coney's humour never failed to shock her, though her very being sometimes struggled to enjoy it.

Charles was silent. Inwardly he was transported with joy. His father, he knew, would not resent this feeling. James Ledwhistle was still puzzled. For his own part he had no yearning to return to the squalid home he had left at the age of 14. How different he thought was England and its people from such as these Virginians. He thought of the injustice, the filth and the greed of England. Outside the jasmine stirred and there drifted on his senses a lingering perfume. Here it was

"Shut the window,"
said Fanny sharply,
and he did.

different: the black-skinned natives with their silky hair and even teeth. It was growing dusky, and faintly on the evening air that was heavy with scent of flowers came the sound of a voice uplifted in song. The voice was rich and throbbed with feeling.

Oh, Masser lying on the hard brown cross,
Massers a-dying and we canna help.

The sky is growing heavy, it is blackening with its loss,
And that dear head is drooping,
It's a-drooping on de cross.

And then there swelled on the breeze a chorus of other throats:

Jesus oh Jesus, his head is drooping now,
Jesus, oh Jesus, we canna let yer die.
Oh, Masa, can't you see us crying?
Youse are going upward, youse are lifting up de sky.

The little room was in darkness now and the flowered curtains swayed gently. Outside there was gathering a little group. Charles caught the gleam of a polished tooth, the white of a glistening eye and a shiny patch on an ebony skin.

'Draw the curtains,' said Fanny sharply, and he did.

Chapter 35

Ernest Ledwhistle ushered his son and nephew Charles Coney into the office of the firm of Ledwhistle and Coney. James was aghast at the magnificence of the surroundings. The polished woodwork, the burnished scuttle, the sparkling blackness of the grate and the bubble-like clarity of the windows overlooking the busy street.

Ernest smiled proudly as he said, 'One day, boys, this firm will be as great as my father made his.'

'But sir,' cried Charles, 'did you know the Pentworth lawyers? Were you a relation or an acquaintance of long standing?'

'I have never met them in my life,' was the answer. 'They have completely disappeared too, but they're genuine enough.'

He looked round with a long-drawn-out sigh of expectancy, as if he half hoped to see the disapproving face of Old Jacob Steinhouse staring at him from behind the half-opened door.

Charles sat down at a desk whose top, gleamed and burnished, waited for him. James was not so willing to adapt himself to a desk. He had last night met his grandmother and the incident had both sickened and revolted him. Ernest had not moved into their new house yet, and she sat among her squalid surroundings. They shared their house with a family of 9: a father and 8 children. James remember going into the back parlour. The dingey light that filtered sluggishly through the window curtains lighted on a cage above a chair. The stench was horrible, and as he gazed with hot eyes the green parrot squawked loudly. And then he had seen his grandmother, Mary Ledwhistle. With what horror he saw the hair-rimmed eyes, the red amber light in those bright pupils, which were sparkling with the very emptiness of their gaze. The lips were drawn up and yellow, her chin low and hanging. Her face was covered in brown freckles and there were large bags under the visionless eyes. Her white hair, grey with dirt, hung round her ears. A drab shawl covered her shoulders and a shapeless colourless sack adorned her body. A disgusting pair of slippers covered her old feet, and her fading hands waved uselessly around in the air.

She saw James but took not the slightest notice of him. 'Folly,' she cackled, her eyes taking on an expression that was truly frightening in their intensity. 'Why, what are you squawking for, you foolish bird? Foolish. Feathers aren't green but feathers are yellow — yellow and blue.' She lapsed into silence and then cried out, gasping, 'Blue, yellow, red, grey and black. Purple too. Foolish, foolish. Wise bird, Polly, Polly.'

Then she seemed to take her grandson in. James shrank back from that stare. Ah, the stare of rotting age. You should see that stare, Richard Soleway, and shrink from it also.

She stopped her restless moving, and her stillness was more terrifying than her motion had been the moment before.

'You're Martin?' she screeched. 'You're Martin, aren't you? Andrew,' she wailed, 'quick, here's Andromikey. Quick, Andrew get the irons. Brand it on his forehead. Brand him, burn him!' Then she cried feverishly, 'It's blue and green and yellow, Francis. How naughty, Polly.'

At that moment Ernest had come into the room and the old woman had stopped her rambling. The old head had gone to one side, and she looked not unlike the green parrot, thought James.

124

'This is James, Mother,' said Ernest gently.

The old woman became still again and her eyes seemed to glow like the coal in a watchman's shelter. 'Ernest,' she croaked. 'It's that young Andromikey. He's there, can't you see?'

'Come James,' Ernest had said calmly. 'Her brain has dissolved, poor soul. We will send the servant round with a bottle of port.'

Now James tried to forget her, and settle down to work, for he wanted to make a success of the firm which had landed on their laps, but oh, it was hard to banish his rotting grandmother from his mind, or to forget her strange words.

Chapter 36

We are in another part of the land, in the quiet country lane which leads to the gentle graveyard of St Carthage's. A figure is tottering betwixt the hedgerows, his gnarled hand clutching a stout walking-stick. There is something familiar in his gait, something that we have seen before in those rheumy blue eyes that tremble in the breeze blowing in from the sea.

A child comes across a field from the pleasant pinewoods that grow near to the sandhills, running in his rude petticoats, a nosegay of flowers in his chubby fist. His rusticated feet stumble on a piece of broken bottle and he cries out piteously, then hops to the bank of the lane and sits with the blood of his gashed foot mingling with the petals of his apple-blossom sprays.

The old man stumbles towards him. Shudder, reader, for it is none other than Rupert Bigarstaff, and there is no one abroad in the lane but he and the little damaged lad.

'Come unto me, all ye that are heavy laden,' says Bigarstaff and, taking off his befluffed necktie he kneels on his cracking joints to help the boy.

He is not feigning concern. Those eyes brim with moisture and spill down his careworn cheeks.

'Verily,' he says, 'you are sore wounded.'

Comforted, the child skips off and vanishes.

Can this be the Rupert Bigarstaff we used to know and fear? What miracle has wrought the change in him? That child could have breathed his last in that lane. And why is Bigarstaff not dead, stuck fast in that swamp of quicksand so many years before?

To understand such a reclamation we must return to the past, to that dreadful moment when the sucking quicksands gave beneath his pounding feet.

Chapter 37

He shouted out, a great bellow of fear, and tried to fly out of the bog. But the more he struggled the more he sank, and finally, just as his mouth was on a level with the green slime, his threshing feet touched something. He stood there, hardly daring to breathe, afraid that what was under his boots would shift and he would be utterly lost. He did not doubt that what he perched on was the dead shoulders of the rascally Captain Trevelian. Or perhaps it was wretched, stabbed John Pearson.

Rupert did not pray. It was not in him to do so. But he murmured a line of a hymn that came back to him from his childhood days, and was stilled by it – 'There is a happy land, far, far away.'

Over his head the clouds were black and heavy, and a few spots of rain began to fall, hitting the green surface of the swamp in front of his nose. He could hear shouts in the distance. He wondered if he would die standing up, the skin falling from his face and his skull bleaching under the fierce noonday sun that would continue to blaze in the heavens when he was no more but gone to that happy land. 'You are doomed to hell eternal,' whispered the wind in the trees. 'There is no happy land for the likes of you.'

It was growing dark now, and as he peered ahead wraiths appeared on the edge of the swamp, holding out mocking arms. There was the young girl he had pushed into the murky waters of the Thames, her locks still streaming water, her face contorted with hatred of him. There was the sunny-haired sailor whom he had consigned to a watery grave so long ago, his knuckles still bright with blood from the cruel stamping against the stone. 'Hell eternal,' they echoed, and their voices rose to an eerie scream as the wind gathered gale force. Mercifully, Rupert Bigarstaff lost consciousness.

He had no idea how long it was he had been in a faint, and when he came to for a moment he feared he was indeed in hell. Jagged lightning zipped across the black sky, illuminating the jagged trees and vegetation, and booms of thunder rolled round his head. The very swamp seemed to be bubbling with unrest, as the rain fell in curtains across the island. He felt moisture lilting against his face, filling his ears. He screamed over and over. And then, suddenly, he found himself floating on his back, looking up at a scarlet flash. He was being carried along by some flood. Again he fainted.

When he woke up the second time he was on dry land, firm land, though soggy from the storm, and already dawn was lighting up the area in which he lay. He realised it was the sea that had flooded in pushed by the violence of the storm to cover the swamp and thus free him in a miraculous manner. He knelt and gave thanks to God, a penitent after all the awful years of sin, his heart full of appreciation to the merciful Lord.

A flash of silver caught his eye, somewhere on his left shoulder. He touched it – and it was his own hair, turned snow white in one ghastly night.

Chapter 38

He did not find it easy to be good. It was not all plain sailing. Two weeks after his salvation from death, the bodies of four sailors were washed up on the beach, their faces contorted with dire horror. Obviously they had tried to get away on some makeshift raft and had drowned in the storm. When he saw them he felt no pity for them and would have left them where they lay to rot, but then he could not sleep that night and had fearful dreams. He imagined he was again in the swamp, being pulled down, down, and woke with the sweat running into his scared eyes.

In the morning he dug a big hole and buried the sailors and stuck a branch on top of the mound and whispered some rough words over their burial. 'Forgive me, Lord,' he said. 'I cannot turn over a new leaf in a few short weeks. Give me more time.'

Once, he saw a turtle struggling on its back in the heat, its short legs waving incompetently. After many hours it managed to right itself and begin to crawl away in a weakened condition. He was about to run forward and upturn it again when an inner voice warned him of his wrong thinking.

After about a year, or so he took it to be, for time went neither slow nor fast on the island and he had no Big Ben to toll the hours away with its booming notes, he was walking along the causeway when he heard a commotion in a thicket. When he went to investigate he saw a mongoose caught in a sort of trap made by an accidental creeper which had bound

The mongoose returned
the next night, and
for many nights to come.

the beast to a tree. He was about to walk on and leave it to its long fate when he paused. Was this a test from the Lord? Carefully he unwound the thick creeper and released the mongoose which flapped off at once.

Afterwards, though he dared not admit it out loud, he felt he had been foolish. He should have killed it for fresh meat, if a bird is meat. Then two days later, when he was sitting by his lonely camp-fire, chewing the last of the tobacco which had remained in his pocket when he had first been shipwrecked, a shadow fell across the sand and he saw the mongoose sitting there, looking at him. He said nothing. He gave no sign that he saw the bird. When he lay down to sleep he knew that the thing was still there, eyeing him with bald eyes.

In the morning the bird had gone, and he felt sad. It returned that night and every night for years to come, and though they never spoke Rupert and he became friends, and it was a bad day when the mongoose finally died of old age and was buried under a banyan tree in the far corner of the island. Then he did weep, freely and without shame, and he sang a long hymn in memory of that faithful feathered comrade.

Chapter 39

Seven years passed before two brigs sailed towards the island. It was the oil men come to stake their claims and dig for the precious liquid. Fortunately all the oil was on one side of the island and Rupert Bigarstaff was able to avoid such unwanted company. He did not feel he was ready to join the land of the living and clung to his solitude.

Sometimes the oil men thought they glimpsed a shadowy figure watching them from a distance, but though they sent out search parties they never found anyone and the captains wrote in their logs that it was probably just a mirage they had seen.

Only once did Rupert Bigarstaff fall from grace. One night he heard the noise of roistering in the distance, and creeping forward on his belly spied the oil men round their camp-fire, drinking from brandy bottles. His mouth watered and his head swam. If only he could get hold of a drink. He waited till they had fallen into a stupor. Then, flitting like a bat, he swooped down and bore off a bottle in his nerveless fingers.

For two days and nights he drank, and his stomach revolted, for it was a long time since a drop had passed his lips. He was afraid he would shout out and caper in his drunkenness, and he bound his mouth with leaves, and tied himself by the foot to a tree when the bottle was empty. It was a ghastly time for him. He got the shudders and the wraiths of his past misdemeanours returned tenfold and danced round him jeering, pointing their skinny fingers and hinting of a devilish revenge.

When the drink had worn off he made a solemn vow, kneeling on the sand and clasping his trembling hands. 'I will not touch the stuff again,' he said. 'By all that's holy I am now cured.' After twenty-one years he decided that the time had come for him to return to England. He wanted to die in the pleasant churchyard in which Old Andrew Ledwhistle had long been laid to rest. Accordingly, he gathered his belongings together and cleaned out the leafy bower which had been his home for so long, and lingering for one last moment at the graveside of the mongoose to murmur goodbye, he went across the island to the oil men.

They were very surprised to meet him, and at first thought he was mad because he spoke like the Bible, and had forgotten any other words. After a good wash and a haircut they put him on the next brig and despatched him homewards.

Chapter 40

Now, his long voyage was over and he was home. Secure in the knowledge that he had been kind to a fellow human being, even one so small and insignificant as the child with the bloody foot, Rupert Bigarstaff continued on his way down the lane towards the church.

The sun was declining, casting ruddy beams in long flakes on the slumbering graveyard. It was a Norman church, and he thought of those warring men who had come to foreign shores and vanquished the population. Along this quiet lane they had trod their marauding way, spears flashing in the moonlight, elk horns curved in their brutal helmets.

'How long, O Lord,' he murmured. 'How long until men will learn to love each other and forsake their foolish ways?' But answer came there none.

Old Andrew's grave was covered all over with ivy. There was a statue of an angel with a broken wing poised in mid-flight over the puny stretch of tomb.

Rupert Bigarstaff was very tired. He had come a long distance, and the ways of men exhausted him. How easy it would be if he could give up the ghost now on this spot and return to his Maker. He knelt in the grass, his old soul swooning. A little breeze rustled the pine-trees. 'Hell,' they sighed. 'Hell waits.'

'No,' he cried aloud. 'I have paid for my sins. I demand heaven.'

And then a fearful pain grabbed his breast. He turned white and then blue. Was it all a trick? Was he to die cheated of his just reward? Had he sacrificed a life of enjoyment to the outworn story of a man on a cross?

He pitched forward, and as he did so the scarlet flames roared towards his proud soul. God is not mocked, reader! He knows what true repentance is, and what is not.

Chapter 41

Richard Soleway walked briskly down the little country lane. He was a heavier, more self-satisfied Richard – or no, perhaps that is being too harsh. Enough to say he was 75 years of age. Side-whiskers did not adorn his face, neither a growth of beard. His eyebrows, far from being bushy, were flat and scanty. A lifting of his bowler would have disclosed as bald a dome as any.

The evening was drawing to a close, and it was a time when darkness wrestled with dusk for the upper hand. It was a time too when country places seem to grow fanciful. Yes, that is the word, fanciful. The dark pines rustled darkly and, in the long rank grass, leaves whispered among themselves. As Richard turned a bend he seemed to go slower, and it was as if a weight was on his legs. Tap, tap, tap went the sharp pointed stick on the gravel, and St Carthage's was before him. Rupert Bigarstaff had found the lonely graveyard vaguely beautiful, but now, as dark shadows played on the great stone walls, it gave an impression of age and faint terror. Through its trees Richard caught the glint of the sea, and the departing sun lying white and wan, after its golden splendour on the edge of it. Softly he trod the grass and entered the yard. He would have strode on but something seemed to arrest him. On he went to the porch and, scarcely breathing, lifted the iron rung on the church door. It swung open and Richard stepped inside. Oh, how desolate it was. The rows and rows of empty pews, the dark curtains drawn before the altar. The sun with its dying palpitation rested heavily on the edge of the window, but had not the strength to peep within. Clank, clank went Soleway's footsteps. No scent of incense was on the air. No jewelled robe, no costly silver candle-holder was there, but God was here for all that and like a child Richard felt hushed and at peace. When the hollow notes of the vicar ring out, and the rows of people in their Sunday best listen with shut hearts, when one looks around to see what Mr Clarkson's niece is wearing and when people walk with pompous steps into their family pew, then Soleway was a stranger to the Lord's house. But now, when the clergyman is absent and no one's chatter distracts him, when he can walk about and need not to his knees bend, then was Richard Soleway at home.

He gazed with clear eyes at the brass cross that swung above him, small and shining. Then, turning, he left and came into the burial ground. All among the ivy he wended his way. As he saw the blackened monument to Andrew Ledwhistle he became aware of the body of a man flung across it. He dropped to one knee as he feverishly turned the old man over. Somehow, even before he saw those eyes, Richard knew who it would be.

'God,' he whispered as he gazed at Rupert Bigarstaff. The white hair hung over the small ears in jagged sprays. The lips were bloodless and the eyes were wide open and oh so cold. Green and cold and dead. Dead and cold and green.   With a shudder Richard let the lifeless old frame drop. Stumbling and cursing, he ran to the gate. Sobbing, he wrenched it open and ran down the road. Cold and Green and Dead. Dead ... Cold. He reached the vicarage path.

When the Reverend Peter Whit opened his door, he was fallen upon almost savagely by Richard Soleway.

'My dear man,' cried Whit, as he was shaken by the lapels till the teeth shook in his head. He was a big man and he was a

He feverishly turned
the old man over.

strong man, but he had to be a clever man to stem Soleway's hysteria.

When he had succeeded in doing so, Soleway was drawn into the back parlour. Peter Whit was a bachelor, and he lived without any servants. Therefore his room was essentially mannish. A grate held a coal fire, which was crackling and spitting. A cover with a green border hung over the mantelpiece, while above it a three-cornered mirror was fixed. On either side of the grate, high up, was a shelf of books with curtains read to draw. In front of this was an old armchair, and a desk stood in the corner. On the mantelpiece was a queerly carved group of tiny statues and several Toby jugs. A warm rug lay by the hearth edge, and worn lino covered the rest. Seated on the armchair was a large dog, with ponderous chops. She was evidently a bitch, for a litter of puppies rolled and squeaked over her.

'Now what exactly has startled you, my dear sir?' Whit asked, his keen eyes noting the old man's prosperous appearance. He wondered rather ashamedly if this gentleman could be persuaded to subscribe for the annual school treat for the village boys.

'Out there,' whispered Richard, 'out there.' His hands clutched his coat hem and he shook uncontrollably. 'There's Bigarstaff and his eyes are cold and green out there.'

'Out where, who's out there?'

'Rupert Bigarstaff, in the graveyard and he's dead.'

Whit shot to his feet. 'Where? Quick.'

But Soleway only moaned and cursed. Peter Whit ran out of the house. He did not wait to go round to the gate, but squeezed through the fence. His eyes caught a white face and he knew Richard Soleway had spoken the truth.

Chapter 42

Charles Coney held tight to the shoulder of his son Colin.

'This,' he said, 'this is Ernest, son.'

Colin Coney put out his hand.

'How do you do,' he said embarrassedly.

Ernest Ledwhistle, the great-grandson of Andrew Ledwhistle, was not so shy. He was a well-built boy some 13 years of age and free from timidness. 'Hallo,' he said.

'Well,' stammered Charles, 'take your cousin to his room, son.'

When the two had gone he turned to his wife. 'You know,' he said, 'it is a shame, Sally. That boy is hiding his real feelings very well.'

Sally pushed a strand of wavy hair from off her brow. 'I know,' she said softly. 'I only wish James could do the same. He's broken-hearted. Not that I blame him. Elsie was the best wife any man could have.'

Charles sat down and drew out a letter. 'I got a letter from Robert Straffordson this morning,' he said. Seeing his wife's disinterested attitude, he went on: 'You know, Sally, Victor Radenstone's son. Surely you've heard of the great Opium hero?'

Sally put down her knitting. 'What is this leading to, dear?'

Charles looked at her sharply. 'It seems the old man wants me to get in touch with old Jane Ledwhistle.'

'Whatever for?' cried Sally, her hands for once idle in her

141

lap. 'How very comical. How's he getting on in that tropical island of his?'

Charles smiled that slow, slow smile of his. 'As far as I can make out, very well indeed. He's not alone, though, for the miners' families are with him. He was very cut up when Radenstone died. Must have been getting on for 89.'

Sally settled down to her work once more while her husband went outside to talk in the garden with James, his cousin, father of the young Ernest. The letter remained on the chair and Sally gently picked it up. Robert Straffordson, Jane Ledwhistle, Ernest, Old Andrew, Martin Andromikey – what a lot of suffering had been known in Charles's family. His uncle's partner's ruthless ruin of the firm, whose downfall had been the tragic death of Old Andrew. Robert Straffordson, the legless old man who had been the son of the man who had helped to reunite Anna Mansall with her loved one. Jane, the one-time music player, now a silent old woman, sister of Francis, that drunkard and destitute man who ever came to call on Charles for money. Strange that one man could cause such suffering and death!

James came into the room. About 50, he was floridly handsome, and very grey. His face was lined and white, for the death of his wife had shocked him greatly.

'Sorry Sally,' he said with an effort, as Charles's wife jerked her head up in startled amazement. 'What were you thinking about?'

'About Martin Andromikey,' answered Sally. 'Think of him, James. Think what he did to your father – to Old Andrew and his wife.'

James sank wearily into a chair and pressed the tips of his fingers together. 'Yes,' he said heavily. 'Poor father. But you know, Sally, he's been rewarded now, hasn't he? Think of the firm. Think of it.'

'He'd paid dearly enough for it, though, didn't he?' put in

Sally, her eyes pools of brown.

James passed a hand across his brow. 'Ah well,' he said slowly, 'it's all over now. All the worry and trouble I mean. Still, I'd like to know where Martin is.'

Martin Andromikey himself was still mouldering in a watery grave, but the bogus Martin, alias Richard Soleway, was seated in an old armchair. He sat gazing into the dying embers that had been a fire and wondered. Now and then a more healthy coal would leap into sudden life and throw the watcher's face into sharp relief.

'Gasper Liverwick,' he murmured, 'Victor Radenstone, Rupert Bigarstaff — they've all gone. And it will be me next.' His head nodded as if stressing the remark.

A coal fell into the grate, dangerously near the carpet, but he paid no heed. His hand went to his pocket bringing forth a key. Slowly he got to his feet and made his way to a cabinet that lay set in the wall. Click, the lock released its steely grip, and the door was open. Putting his hand inside, Richard brought forth a small oblong box. This he also unlocked and drew out an envelope. It was addressed in yellowish writing to Ernest Ledwhistle. He stumbled once more to his chair clasping the confession to him. Once more he took to musing. And as he fell asleep there was a smell of smoke in his nostrils.

Neighbours of Richard Soleway's were rudely awakened that night by the shout of 'Fire'. Standing in their groups, unable to stop its course, they watched the flames spread. And when the morning came, and the charred ashes were blown softly in all directions the unrecognisable body of Richard was found. In his hand was a bundle of ashes. So Richard Soleway perished, and with him his confession.

Chapter 43

And now, dear readers, I have reached the end of my story, and all that remains is for me to put down my pen and first think of a suitable patching up. I will now gather the loose threads of my story together and ease your minds on a few things.

First, James Ledwhistle settled down happily secure in the knowledge that his son would enter the business. Jane Ledwhistle received vaguely poetical letters from Robert Straffordson and wondered. Young Ernest grew into a fine young man, and eventually married, later having 5 sturdy sons to his credit. So, to finish on a faintly sad note, let us journey to St Carthage's, where lie the graves of 4 men. The ivy rustles softly, and on the air steals the sound of an organ. And looking upward through the arch of trees, with the sea beyond we find that there are no clouds in the sky.

The End

Begun June 1st, 1946

18th August 1946